## SECRET ADMIRER

*It was very pleasant to have him so friendly, the boy whom all the girls had admired. And Natalie couldn't blame them. She had admired him herself always. She had seldom had the pleasure of going to a school game . . . but she had often stood at the schoolroom window at recess and watched the boys practicing in the yard below. And always she had singled out Chris as the most finished player, and exulted in the way he led them all, and they deferred to him.*

*Well, now she was enjoying a pleasant little contact with one whom she could have enjoyed as a friend if their circumstances in life had been different, but she must not let her head get turned by it. After all, they were born into different worlds. . . .*

Tyndale House books by Grace Livingston Hill.
Check with your area bookstore for these best-sellers.

# THE PATCH OF BLUE

**LIVING BOOKS** ®
Tyndale House Publishers, Inc.
Wheaton, Illinois

This Tyndale House book
by Grace Livingston Hill
contains the complete text
of the original hardcover edition.
NOT ONE WORD
HAS BEEN OMITTED.

Living Books is a registered trademark of Tyndale
House Publishers, Inc.

Printing History
J. B. Lippincott edition published in 1932
Tyndale edition/1992

Cover artwork copyright © 1992 by Steven Stroud

Library of Congress Catalog Card Number 92-80163
ISBN 0-8423-4809-3

Printed in the United States of America

99  98  97  96  95  94  93  92
 8   7   6   5   4   3   2   1

CHRISTOPHER Walton closed the hymn book, put it in the rack, carefully adjusted his mother's wrap on her shoulders as she sat down, arranged the footstool at her feet comfortably, and then sat back and prepared to get himself through the boredom of the sermon time.

Chris had no idea of trying to listen to the sermon. He never even pretended to himself that he was listening. He carried his tall, good-looking self to church regularly because it was a thing required by both Father and Mother that the household should attend church, but his soul was as far away as possible from the dim religious light of the sanctuary. Nobody suspected of course that behind his handsome polite exterior the world was rushing gayly on in his thoughts. It would have been a most astonishing thing if the world in which his thoughts were revelling could have suddenly appeared in church. It would have created quite an uproar. Sometimes it was a football game with the grandstand rooting wildly and he himself making a glorious touchdown. Sometimes it was a party he had attended the night before, with jazzy music stealing all through his thoughts. Sometimes it was a medley of his own plans for life, when he saw himself alternately writing a book that should set the world on fire; or becoming a central figure on the floor of the stock exchange; or again a wealthy stock broker who would finally get to the place where he could give great sums to charity and education.

But none of these things figured in his thoughts this morning. His mind was full of college. Three weeks more and he expected to be gone from this pew, gone back to college life. He drew a breath of secret satisfaction as he remembered that a college student could do as he pleased about attending divine service. If he had important lessons to study, or wasn't feeling up to the mark, he could just stay away. There would be no compulsion. Oh, of course, there was no real compulsion at home. Nobody would have forced him to go if he had taken a stand against it perhaps; yet his father's expectation, and the grieved look in his mother's eyes, were as good as a law to him, and he would have felt most uncomfortable and out of harmony with his family if he had attempted to cut church here. And Chris loved his family. He enjoyed pleasing his father and mother even though it was sometimes a bore.

His father was getting old, he reflected with a pang. His hair was deeply silvered. There were heavier lines coming into his kindly face. Chris was still a little anxious over the look that had come into his face at the breakfast table as he finally yielded to their pleas that he stay at home this morning and nurse up the blinding headache that had made it impossible for him to eat his breakfast.

Chris settled back comfortably in his father's place at the head of the cushioned pew and reflected briefly on what a pleasant family he had. Nothing must ever be allowed to happen to his family! He paid them each brief tribute. Such a sweet mother, natural pink in her cheeks, and a delicate look of refinement and peace about her. His sister Elise, pretty and stylish and smart. She was off at a weekend house party to-day and he missed her from her corner of the pew. They had always been good comrades. He was going to miss her when he went back to college.

College! Ah, now he was off! College! It would be his senior year. It was going to be great! Dad had been just wonderful about it. He had arranged to have him take one of the very best rooms in the whole dorm. And it was practically settled that Walt Gillespie was to be his room mate in place of that dub, Chad Harmon. They were to have a suite, two bedrooms and a spacious sitting room between. Of course there were many students who couldn't afford an outfit like that. And Mother had given up one of her very finest oriental rugs, the one he had always admired the most, for his floor. Of course she would have a new one in its place but he knew she loved this blue one, yet wanted him to have it. She said they wanted his last year to be the best of all. Then Dad was making a generous donation to their new fraternity building; and there had been a hint dropped that he would be suggested for president of their chapter next semester. Dad had been awfully generous in the way of money, too, said he wanted him to have everything during his college life because one went to college only once. Dad had been pleased that he had been popular in his father's old fraternity. Of course it was Dad's influence that had gotten him in here at all right at the first. They were a terribly exclusive bunch. It was wonderful having a father who was well off and able to put one into the front ranks of things.

And then, the crowning joy of all, Dad was going to let him have a car, one of the very best, to take with him. He had picked it out and it was coming to-morrow morning. He was to take it out on a trial trip alone, and try it out thoroughly before the final deal was made. But it was practically bought already, for he was sure he would find nothing wrong with it. It was a great car.

The shining new car in all its glory of flashing chromium and deep blue body rolled slowly down the aisle past his pew and let him study it as the minister rose in the pulpit to announce and introduce a visiting preacher that morning. Chris was so interested in his car that he hardly heard what was going on, scarcely noticed the stranger on the platform.

Chris was thinking how he would take Gilda Carson out for a ride to-morrow after he had had a good long tour by himself. Gilda was rather highhat and always boasting about Bob Tyson's car and how he had taken her here and there. But Bob Tyson's car wasn't worth mentioning in the same breath with his new one. Gilda would boast about his now, he was sure.

Not that he cared so much what Gilda thought or did. She wasn't especially his girl, but it had been a bit irksome having her always talking about Bob's wonderful car. Well there wasn't going to be anything wrong with his new car. It was a wonder. Such a purring engine, free-wheeling, adjustable seats, marvelous shock absorbers, and above all, speed! The car was doing eighty and even ninety now, up and down the stately aisles of the church, and Chris sat with a saint-like expression on his face and watched it. He almost wondered that the people about him did not turn and look after it in admiration.

Suddenly a new voice broke into his meditations. The minister had introduced the stranger.

He was announcing his text now—two texts. "Oh give thanks unto the Lord for He is good!" and "How can we sing the Lord's song in a strange land?"

Chris recognized the first text as a part of the responsive reading they had just had, but the second seemed a little bit out of the ordinary, and he wondered idly what it could possibly have to do with the first. The opening words of the preacher's sermon arrested his attention for an instant:

"It is easy enough to thank God when everything is going well and we have all that we want in our lives. The true test of a thankful heart is to be able to sing praise when things are going all wrong. When we have lost our money or our friends or are disappointed in our dearest ambitions, or when we are in a strange unhappy environment, then we cry out 'How can we sing the Lord's song in a strange land?'"

That was about all Chris heard of that sermon, and he only wondered idly a moment about it before he drifted back into his own thoughts. He averred to himself that of course it was ridiculous to expect anybody to be thankful for sorrow and disaster, for poverty and sickness and loss. The minister seemed to be giving an instance of someone who had said he was grateful for every trouble that had ever come to him, and through his disappointments had learned to praise the Lord for every one. Well, that was absurd. No one could thank the Lord for unhappiness. He was thankful that his life was laid in pleasant surroundings, and he paused long enough in his reflections to give a quick thanksgiving for his home, his parents, his pleasant environment, the happy college days that still lay before him, his new car—and then he was off again into the anticipations of his senior year at college and what he had to do before he went back. He tabulated different items mentally on his fingers, things he must not forget. Not the least among them was the trial of the new car to-morrow, and presently the car was rolling up and down the aisle again before his happy vision, and the minister with his absurd message about being glad for unhappiness was utterly forgotten.

He had arranged a full program for the next few days when at last the closing hymn was announced, and he found the place for his mother and arose with relief to join in the hymn of praise. He noticed with a vague annoyance that there was a line in the hymn that conveyed that same illogical suggestion about giving thanks for trouble that the minister had suggested in the beginning of his sermon. But he raised his voice a little louder when it came to the refrain of praise, and steadily thought of all the thrilling joys of his own life with a true thanksgiving. He certainly was grateful that the lines had fallen to him in such pleasant places, and just now he was more than all grateful that the service was over and he would soon be free to go back to the delightful details of every day living.

Out in the lovely summer day at last he drew a breath of relief and began to talk eagerly to his mother about the new curtains she was going to select the next day for his college room. He had decided ideas of just what he wanted, built upon a college room of a famous athlete he had seen last spring.

Chris was glad that his father's headache seemed to be better, and that the dinner table was a cheerful place, with all the things he liked best to eat. His father seemed a bit grave and silent but he attributed that to the headache, for he responded smiling to anything that was said. Chris tried to persuade himself that he had only imagined those lines of care on his father's face. He talked eagerly of his new car, and his father seemed pleased and promised to take a drive with him if he would come down to the bank between eleven and twelve o'clock next day.

Monday morning Chris came whistling down the

stairs with a glad light in his eyes. His mother stood in the hall just below him and he paused at the foot of the stairs to stoop and touch a light kiss on her forehead. Such a pretty little mother! But he knew just what she was going to say and he wished to forestall it. She was a little peach of a mother of course, but she always had been afraid of things, and he was so full of his own joy this morning that he felt a little impatient toward her fears.

"Oh, Chris, you will be careful, won't you?" she implored, just as he had known she would do.

"Sure, Muzzie. I'm always careful. Why, what's the idea? You act as though I had never driven before."

"But, a new car, Chris, that's different. You don't know how it will act. And a new kind that you have never driven before. That free wheeling. I'm afraid of it. You don't know how to work it. They tell me it's quite different from other driving. I wish you'd take a service man along with you the first day or two."

Chris laughed gayly.

"Well, I like that! A service man! I think I see myself! Why, Mud, you know Uncle Eben's car was just like this one and I drove it for him all the time he was here, every day for two weeks. But, Mother, seriously, you must stop worrying about me. I'm not a kid any more. I'm a man. This is my last year at college, remember. And besides, there isn't a car made that I can't drive. Why do you suppose I've hung around Ross Barton's garage all these years if not for that? I'm considered a good driver. Why don't you go along with me and prove it? I'll give you a good ride, and leave you wherever you say, then you will have more confidence in me."

"Oh, I can't, Chris, I have a committee meeting here at the house this morning. But you won't be late for lunch, will you? You know I'll be worried."

The boy stooped and silenced her with a real kiss on her soft anxious lips now.

"Now, look here, Mother," he said earnestly, "you've just got to stop worrying. You're just making trouble for yourself. Besides, I'm stopping at the bank at eleven for Father and you know he'll come back on time. You've got him well trained. Sure you don't want to go along just for a little spin? Well, come on out and look at the car anyway. Did you see it yet from the window? Look!"

He flung the front door open.

"There! Isn't that a winner! Isn't it the niftiest car you ever saw? Long clean sporty lines. Dad was great to do all this for me. It's going to make all the difference in the world in my college life having this car."

His mother smiled indulgently with a wistful look in her eyes, and patted his arm.

"Your father feels that you deserve it, Chris," she said lovingly. "We want you to get the greatest enjoyment possible out of your last year in college."

She stood in the open doorway and watched him drive away, thinking what a happy lot was hers with such a son. Then she turned with a bit of a sigh of anxiety, and yet a smile, and went back to her pleasant sheltered life thinking how good God had been to her.

Chris drove out into the clear September morning, his face alight with satisfaction. Down through the pleasant village street of the pretty suburb where he had been born. He wanted first of all to ride around the old familiar streets and get used to the idea that this wonderful car was his.

As he thrilled to the touch of the new wheel he remembered that first old Ford he had bought for ten dollars. He had had to tinker with it for three weeks before it would run. He had been so happy with it then, till the kindly policeman who had known him all his young life stopped him because he was too young to drive and had no license. But he never dreamed that day that only a few short years more and he would be driving one of the best cars that was made, and thrilling to the thought that it was all his own.

It was practically his own now. Dad would see to the red tape of the purchase to-morrow morning. He had promised. And then he would drive it back to the home garage and it would be his. It made him feel a man to think of it. He had a sudden memory of his first express wagon and how serious life had looked to him as he had taken it out that first morning after Christmas, on the street, and showed it to his playmates. And his first bicycle! Dad had always been so good to him, getting him everything he wanted. How he loved that wheel!

But boy! It had been nothing like this first car! This was great!

Skimming along with the top down, and the wind in his hair! There was nothing like it!

He was skirting the edge of the little grove just outside of town now where they used to have the High School picnics. The trees were golden, with here and there a vivid coral one. They were early in turning. The yellow leaves against the blue of the autumn sky filled him with an ecstasy. He wished he had someone to talk to who would understand, yet he felt that it would be impossible to put into words what he was feeling. College and car, and the glory of the day all mixed up in his soul. Boy! It was great!

He whirled back into town again and traversed the streets, going slowly by his own house and waving to his mother whose face he could see at the window, just to give her confidence in his driving. His mother waved back to him. She was a great little mother! She was a pretty good sport after all, fearful as she was. Some mothers would have made a terrible kick at having their sons go off to college with a high powered car. Mothers were always so afraid of accidents.

There was Natalie Halsey. He would pick her up and take her for a spin. She had her arms full of bundles and would perhaps be glad of the lift. He had never had much to do with Natalie although they had been in the same class in High School. She was a quiet shy girl, always hurrying off home right after school, and never going to any of the parties or High School affairs, a bit shabby too, and with very few friends among the High School clique. Had he heard that her father died this summer? He wasn't quite sure. It would be better not to mention it. He hadn't seen Natalie for a year or two. He couldn't just remember when it was.

He drew up along side of the girl and called out pleasantly:

"Hello, Natalie, want to ride? I'm going your way."

Natalie turned with a delighted smile and surrendered her heavy bundles as he sprang out and took them from her.

"That will be wonderful!" she said turning a tired smile upon him, and he wondered that he had never noticed before what blue eyes she had. "I was just wondering whether I could get these things home. I twisted my arm yesterday and it aches so I could hardly hold on to everything."

"You oughtn't to try to carry such loads," reproved Chris in a grown-up tone. "Why didn't you have them sent?"

"Well, you see the chain stores don't deliver," said Natalie frankly, "and we can't afford to go to any other." She laughed gayly as if it were a joke and he looked at her with a wondering pity. He had never realized before that people who were decent at all had to consider such trivial matters. It embarrassed him. He hastened to change the subject and took naturally the one uppermost in his mind which was college.

"You're going back to college this fall I suppose? I forget where you went."

Natalie laughed again, this time wistfully.

"No such luck for me," she said. "I went for two years to the University, but last year Mother was too sick to leave, and this year—well—I oughtn't to complain," she added brightly, "I've just got a job and I'm very fortunate in these hard times."

"A job!" said Chris in dismay, and looked at her wonderingly, why, she seemed just a kid out of High School! So slender and frail looking!

"You know my father died last spring," added Natalie sadly, "I needed a job badly."

"Oh, I'm sorry!" said Chris. He felt he was making a bungle of things. He recalled suddenly that Natalie had not been at the High School commencement exercises three years ago. Someone had been sick. Her essay which had received honorable mention had been read by someone else. Poor kid! She must have been having a rotten time.

"I just got the job," confided Natalie almost eagerly, "I'm to be cashier at the chain store on the corner of Park Avenue. I'm so pleased."

There was a ring to her voice that told of anxiety and need and Chris looked at her wonderingly, pityingly.

"Oh, I say," said Chris as they neared her home, "wouldn't you like to take a little spin? You don't have to go in yet do you? I've just got this new car and I'm trying her out. Want to go?"

"Oh, I'd love to," said Natalie breathlessly, "but I've got to get right home. You see my mother's been very sick again and I've left her all alone this morning. It was only a bad case of flu but she's very weak and I don't like to leave her long. My sister had to go on an errand. But the car is wonderful and I thank you for this much of a ride. I shall remember it a long time."

He helped her out and carried her bundles to the door of the plain little house for her, and suddenly thought of the contrast between this home and his own. There was something touching and lovely in the way Natalie thanked him. Her voice was sweet and womanly. He felt a deep discomfort at the thought that this pretty frail girl had to work in a grocery store and make change for all kinds of people.

The discomfort lasted as he spun away from the door into the bright September day again. He half wished he had not picked Natalie up and got to know the unhappiness in her life. He couldn't do anything about it of course.

He whirled into another street and there was Betty Zane coming around the corner.

"Hello, Betts!" called Chris. "Wantta ride in my new buggy!"

"Oh, boy! Do I?" replied Betty eagerly clambering in without waiting for him to get out and help her, and they whirled away into the sunshine.

Betty was pretty and stylish and a great chatterbox. Betty admired the car and in the same breath told of one as wonderful that Bruce Carson had just bought. Betty had much gossip to tell of the different members of the old High School class, and threw out many hints as to parties to which she might be induced to go with the boy that got in the earliest request. Betty talked of college and what she expected to do there, decried the fact that Chris was not attending a co-educational college where they might continue their acquaintance, openly said she would like more rides in his wonderful new roadster, and left him reluctantly when it was time for him to go for his father.

Chris had quite forgotten Natalie and her difficulties when he rode down town toward his father's bank. His mind was full of the things that Betty Zane had told him. When he closed his eyes he could see the bright red speck that had been Betty's little sharp painted lips, and the dancing sarcastic eyes. He still heard ringing in his ears some of the flattery she had handed him. He knew that some of the things Betty had said had been bold, things that his mother would not have liked. But of course Betty was a modern girl. Mother would have to learn that girls were not as when she was young. Then why should he suddenly think of Natalie? She was a girl more like the girls of his mother's day. But then that was probably because she had had no chance in life, no good times. She was old-fashioned, poor thing! But she was nice. Too bad she couldn't have had a better chance!

Then he turned down town and made his way through increasing traffic toward his father's bank.

Within a half a block of the bank he came to a traffic light. As he waited for it to change he noticed an unusual jam in traffic and stretched his neck to discover the cause.

Then he saw that a long double line of people were blocking the sidewalk in front of the bank and surging out into the street, right in the way of traffic. What would it mean?

The light flashed green and Chris moved on a few paces nearer to the scene of confusion. There must have been an accident. There were so many people and cars he could not see what was the matter. Then as he drew nearer he saw ugly menacing faces in the crowd, and he heard a rough voice call out:

"There he is, the son of the president, ridin' round in

a five thousand dollar car, while we have to sweat fer our money!" Then a kind of growl passed over the crowd like a roll of muffled thunder, and suddenly a little thick-set man in the crowd picked up a brick from a pile along the curb where the road was being mended and hurled it straight at Chris. It crashed through the beautiful glass of the windshield, barely escaped hitting him in the temple and glanced off through the open window at his left. Chris was too much astonished to even be frightened at first.

But the shattering glass had fallen among the crowd and cut hands and faces here and there, a bit got into someone's eye, and all was confusion. Fists were shaken in his face, angry threats were hurled at him, and Chris was put to it to know what to do, for the car was tight in traffic and he could not move it.

Then suddenly he heard the voice of his friend the policeman at his left.

"Better get out of here quick, Chris," he said in a guarded voice, "start yer engine. I'll make a way fer ya," and the mounted officer of the law rode fearlessly into the crowd hitting this way and that with his club, till the mob separated enough for Chris to go through, escorted by two or three burly policemen who appeared out of the throng. They battled an opening through to the side street that led to the alley back of the bank, but as they turned the corner Chris heard the report of a shot and a bullet whistled by his ear straight through what was left of the windshield. Then Chris knew that he had had a close call.

As he reached the alley back of the bank where he had meant to turn in, the mob surged from the other end of the block coming toward him.

"Get inta that back doorway there quick and lock it

after ya," said the friendly policeman riding close, "I'll look after yer car. Be spry there."

Chris slid from the car and another officer slipped in behind him. Chris sprang to the doorway, but the door was locked. He began to beat upon the door, and the mob with yells of delight surged toward him. He put his shoulder to the heavy door, but he could not even shake it. The crowd were all but upon him, when suddenly without warning the door gave way and he fell across the threshold!

2

CHRIS never knew exactly what happened for the next minute or two. Someone kicked him as he lay there across the threshold, and a cruel blow from a heavy club hit his arm. Someone shouted "Kill him!" and then he heard a policeman's whistle and wild confusion. Someone had caught him from within the door and was pulling him inside the building. Someone else caught his feet from without and pulled. His shoe came off in the struggle. Something hit him on the head with a dull thud. There were wild yells and a sudden blank.

The door was shut when he came to, and he was inside. Anxious faces were about him. He couldn't quite distinguish them but he tried to straighten up from the hard couch where he was lying, and he recognized that he was in the back room of the bank building, a store room for old records and files.

"I'm all right!" he said unsteadily as he tried to stand up, thinking of his father somewhere in the building. Then a memory of his mother came and quite brought him back to his senses. His mother must not hear about this. All her worst fears would be justified. She would never feel safe about him again.

Then came with a pang the thought of his beautiful car. Where was it? Was it ruined? Oh, what had happened anyway? Why was all that mob out there, and what was going on? Had there been an accident? And had they mistaken him for someone else? He was still dazed from the blow on his head.

Someone brought him a glass of water and he drank it slowly trying to remember just what had happened. His blood was beginning to boil with indignation over the indignity done to himself and his car. He was beginning to be furious with himself for not having jumped into that crowd and seized the fellow who had thrown that brick. What was the matter with him anyway that he had weakly submitted to being led away by the police? He should have done some heavy tackling to show that crowd where to get off. What was the use of being a star football player if one couldn't act in a time of emergency? Of course it had taken him by surprise, but he should have done something even so. He turned toward the door with a thought of going out yet and getting somebody, but even as he turned things went black before his eyes, and he caught himself from falling by the headrest.

"Better lie down again," advised an anxious voice that he vaguely identified as one of the cashiers in the bank. Then another put out a kindly hand and tried to lead him to the couch, but the motion brought him back from the confusion of his mind again.

"No, I'm quite all right now, thank you," he said blinking at them. "Where's Dad? I'd like to see Dad."

They looked at one another, whispered, and one of them stepped to the door and tapped. Another whispered conversation and he came back.

"Your father's in consultation but he'll see you in about ten minutes," he said gravely.

Chris sank down on the hard couch again and began to take account of stock. It was then he missed his shoe.

"Say, did that hyena get my shoe?" he asked with a shade of his old grin coming back to his face.

"He sure did!" responded one of the cashiers gravely looking out of the grating above the door. "What's left of it is out there in the alley I guess, but you wouldn't want to wear it. I have an extra pair in the closet. I'll get them. Maybe they will serve you for the time till you can do better."

He brought the shoes and Chris had recovered sufficiently to laugh at the fit of them. He arose trying to get back some of his old assurance and poise. Then someone opened the door to his father's office and beckoned him and he had to throw his whole energy into the effort to walk steadily through that door. He must not frighten his father. He felt a good deal shaken up, but he was all right.

"You're lucky you came off as well as you did," murmured the cashier as he closed the door behind him.

Then Chris walked into his father's presence and stood in dismay. For the bank president was sitting at his beautiful mahogany desk with his head down upon his arms on the desk top and a look of utter despair about his whole drooping figure.

"Dad! What's the matter?" Chris cried in alarm, quickened out of his daze by the sight of the stricken look of his beloved father.

Slowly the father lifted his head, struggled upright in his chair and looked at him with such a ghastly haggard face his son was more alarmed than ever. Why, his hair seemed to have silvered more in the few hours since breakfast, and those deep lines in his face were terrible to see.

"What's the meaning of all this, Dad? Are you sick? Oh, *Dad!*"

His father passed a trembling hand over his forehead and eyes and struggled to make his voice steady.

"No, son, I'm not sick. I'll be all right. It's—just—been a shock of course."

"But—what is it, Dad?" And then with dawning comprehension, "What's the meaning of all that crowd outside in the street? Has something happened? There hasn't been a run on the bank? Dad—*has there?*"

He saw by the look in his father's face that it was true, and sought to find the right word of encouragement.

"But it can't be anything serious can it, Dad? Our bank? *Your* bank?"

"It's serious, son," answered his father huskily. "It couldn't be more so. There's been a traitor at work inside our ranks."

"Oh, Dad! But don't look that way. It'll be righted somehow."

"Yes, it'll be righted," agreed the utterly sad voice humiliated to the depths, "It'll be righted for the depositors I trust. At least they won't lose much, we hope, perhaps nothing in the end. But it means utter ruin for us! For your mother and you and me! For your uncle Ben, and Mr. Chalmers, and the Tryons."

Chris looked perplexed.

"But," he said looking at his father bewildered, "I don't understand why you—"

"No, you don't understand, son. It is too astounding. You couldn't understand. But son, it means that we as officers and directors will have to give up everything in order to satisfy our depositors. It means that even our house and furniture must go, everything that will bring in *any*thing. It means that your mother and I will have no home and no income, and I am too old to begin again, Chris. It couldn't be done!" He ended with a groan, and Chris staggered across the room and laid his hand upon his father's silvered head that was down upon his arms again.

"Never mind, Dad," he found himself saying bravely, over the terrible lump that had come in his throat, "You've got *me*. I can carry on."

The father's answer was another groan, and then he lifted his head and the boy saw that there were tears in his father's eyes.

"You don't understand yet, Chris. It means that I can't send you, my only son, back to college! It means that I can't buy you the car I promised, nor do any of the other things for you and your sister that I've always meant to do. And how are you going to carry on without a college diploma in these days? I can't do a thing for you. *I!* To have failed!"

"There, Dad! Don't feel that way!" said the boy patting his father's arm awkwardly, "what's the difference? I don't mind. I oughtn't to have had a car yet anyway. I—It—" and then suddenly he knew that he must not tell his father what had happened to him and the car as he was coming in. If he was going to be a man and help his father now, that was one thing he would have to take care of himself without his father's help. Whatever he was liable for that had been damaged he would pay himself. Perhaps it would be covered by insurance, he didn't know. But he closed his lips tight and resolved that he would tell nothing about it. His father had enough to bear.

"Look here, Dad!" he began again, "can't you get out of this place and go home? Does Mother know anything about what's happened?"

"I trust not," said the man hoarsely his whole frame shaken by a convulsive sob. "Not yet."

"Well, there, what's the use in taking it so hard? There'll be some way out. Doesn't Mother own our house? Can't you keep that?"

The gray head was shaken solemnly.

"She owns it," he said wearily, "I put it in her name long ago. But only for her need in case of my death. We talked it all over then, about men who did that to protect themselves when they knew they were about to fail. Mother said then, and I know she'll stick by it now, that she wouldn't think of keeping a house when others felt we were in debt to them. It wouldn't be honorable, son. We've got to do the straight thing even though we are penniless."

Chris was silent a moment, taking it all in. Then he answered bravely:

"Sure thing, Dad. Of course we have!" and somehow the father felt a little thrill of comfort from the way the boy said that "we" including himself in the wholesale sacrifice. The father put out his hand and grasped the hand of his boy.

"Thank you for that, son. You're going to stand by, and that'll help a lot. I feel that I'm awfully to blame not to have discovered sooner what was going on, but we'll work it out, somehow, *together!* You've helped me a lot already boy! Now, I'm going out there and speak to the crowd."

"Oh, no, Dad!" cried Chris in quick alarm. "Listen! You mustn't. I've been out there. I know what it's like. The people are seeing red just now. It wouldn't be safe. Wait till to-morrow, Dad. Wait till you've made some kind of a statement in the papers. Wait till the people have cooled off a little."

"No, son! I'm going now. I've got to face the thing

or I couldn't live with myself over night. There are people out there in distress. Widows, and orphans, who trusted me with their all. They've been telephoning all day till I'm nearly crazy. Mrs. Manders, the widow of my old friend. Mrs. Byers, that poor little old paralytic, and those two Johnson sisters sewing their fingers to the bone making clothes for people and putting it all in here for a rainy day. Oh! It's a burden too great to be borne! But I must tell them I'll do my best."

"Oh, but not yet, Dad! Not to-day!"

"Yes, to-day! Now! I couldn't go home and face my wife with it undone. She would expect it of me. She would want it. Don't worry, son, I've sent for a band of police to stand about in the crowd lest there might be some lawless ones. There are always those when there is any excitement."

"You don't understand, Dad. You mustn't go out now. It would be suicidal."

"Yes, I understand. And I must go. You stay here, lad!"

"No, Dad, if you're going out I belong with you!" protested Chris.

"Listen, son, there isn't any danger of course, but if there should be, I'd rather you were safe in here, to take care of Mother."

"No, Dad, she'd want me to stand by you!" declared Chris, linking an arm in his father's.

So they stood when Mr. Chalmers, one of the directors, tapped at the door and entered.

"They've come, Mr. Walton," he said respectfully, almost deprecatingly, "but I wish you'd be persuaded! The chief says he'll do his best but he wishes you wouldn't go to-day."

"Thank you," said the bank president, lifting his distinguished-looking head a trifle in a way that meant he could not be persuaded, "I am ready." Then he looked down at Chris whose young head was thrown back with that same look of determination, and smiled gravely, adding, *"We* are ready."

Mr. Chalmers opened his lips with a glance at Chris to protest, and another director, Mr. Tryon, in the doorway said, half under his breath, "Oh, do you think that's wise?" Then they closed their lips and stood back with respect in their eyes for the father and son. There was that in the eye of each that made it necessary for them to go, and to stand together.

The wild-eyed crowd, milling together, battling for the first place next the great bronze grating of the doors, turning feverish glances toward the entrance, calling out threats now and then, pushing, selfish, almost crushing the few frightened, determined women who had joined themselves to the mob, were suddenly brought to amazement by the unexpected opening of the doors.

Those immediately in front were precipitated into the marble entrance way, falling at the feet of the advancing two, the father and the son.

Two cashiers had opened the doors, swinging them back noiselessly behind the noisy unnoticing crowd, who had stood there for five hours beating upon that door and screaming out threats, and who were now so busy with their own madness that they did not even see the opening doors.

Just an instant the crowd blinked and wavered, as the four bullies who had occupied first place in the doorway rolled backwards upon the floor, then four others were quick to mount over them and clamber on, wild for their rights and their money.

But two officers with clubs quickly beat back the throng and brought them to their senses, and the crowd drew closer and cried out with many voices for a hearing and their money. The women were pleading now with clasped hands and tears rolling down their cheeks. It was a wild scene of confusion, and Chris's heart stood still with the horror and the sadness of it as he stood for that first instant in the doorway until the fallen men could be removed from their way. The pitifulness of life! For the first time in his few short years he realized a little sense of the sorrow and the helplessness of a great part of the world. He had never had a thought before for his fellow men who were not as fortunate as himself. Now he began to see and understand and his heart swelled painfully with the greatness of misery, and the thought that indirectly perhaps his beloved father, and therefore himself also, had been the cause of it. For the first time he realized the reason for that stone which had been flung through his beautiful new windshield a few short minutes before, and for that cry he had not recalled until now: "There he is, the son of the president, riding round in a five thousand dollar car!" He could see how they had felt and he was filled with a new kind of shame.

Then out they stepped, the president of the bank with his only son, and a wild cry burst from the mob in the street. One moment they stood there side by side, then the president of the bank raised his hand and the mob hushed for an instant, just one breathless moment, and while the silence hung in space, before it should break into chaos, Christopher Walton senior spoke:

"Friends": he said, and his voice was steady and clear so that it was heard to the utmost edge of the crowd.

Then from across the street there came a missile, swift and hard and sure, aimed straight for the brave man's face. It was Chris who saw what was coming and drew his father aside just a hair's breadth. The ball of slime and mud hit harmlessly the grill of the door before which he stood, and glanced off, only spattering his face. But even then he did not waver. He merely took out his white handkerchief and wiped away the mud from his cheek and eyes, and then lifted his hand again for silence.

The sheer bravery of the act silenced the crowd again for an instant and while it lasted he spoke.

"Friends, I am here to tell you that you shall get back every penny of your savings just as soon as it is possible. I personally pledge to give up all I have, my home and personal property, and I know the directors will do the same. This thing has come about through a circumstance which is just as surprising and heartbreaking to us as to you, and to the last cent we have we shall make good. We ask you to go quietly to your homes, and within a few days, just as soon as it is physically possible to find out the extent of our trouble and our resources, we shall communicate with every one of our depositors and let them know how soon they may expect their first instalment of what is coming to them. We ask your cooperation, and it is to our mutual benefit to work together."

He paused an instant and glanced down at his son standing so straight and tall beside him, almost reaching his father's height, then he added, with the first smile that had lightened his sorrowful features all that day:

"My son is here beside me to say that if anything happens to his father before this promise is made good, he stands ready to see that it is fulfilled. Isn't that so, Chris?"

"It sure is, Dad," answered the son with a clear ring in his voice.

Then the crowd, always ready to be swayed either way, broke into a cheer, and some of the women openly wept.

Only on the outer edge of the crowd where the policemen were quietly handcuffing a black-browed youth with slime on his hands, was there a low menacing undertone, like a growl of distant thunder.

Then a hand drew the father and son within the sheltering doors again, and most of the crowd turned and drifted slowly, hesitatingly, away.

Sometime later a closed car drove up around the corner of the alley, back of the bank, and took the Waltons and two of the bank directors to their homes; and the region about the bank, and the streets where they had to pass were well patrolled.

Mrs. Walton was in a high state of excitement when they finally arrived at home.

"Where have you both been?" she cried tearfully, "I've been so worried. I thought there had been a terrible accident and you were both killed. I even tried to telephone the bank, but got no answer except that the wire was busy. I thought I should go crazy."

"Oh," said the elder Walton sympathetically, "that was because so many people were calling up constantly. I'm so sorry. I never dreamed that you would be worried yet, and I did not want to tell you until it was necessary, not until I could come home and explain it myself. My dear, we have been passing through terrible times this morning." He passed a frail hand over his furrowed forehead and looked at her with weary eyes. Chris, watching him, seemed to see him suddenly grow old before his eyes. He saw his mother put her hand hastily over her heart in quick premonition and while his father explained about the run on the bank it all swept over him what it was going to mean to his mother to lose her home, and be poor. Gosh, that was tough on Mother! His little pretty mother! It suddenly came to him that he must somehow stand between her and this so great calamity.

Then amazingly he saw her face relax, her fears drop away, her face grow calm, and almost a smile come out upon her lips.

"Oh, is that all?" she said with great relief, "I thought you must have some awful sickness or a stroke, or you were going to have to have a terrible operation."

Suddenly Chris began to laugh.

"Oh, Mother," he cried, "excuse me, but—why!—you're only afraid of the things you imagine, things you get up yourself out of nothing! When it comes to real things, Muz, you've got the nerve. I'll say you're a real little old hero!"

"But Mary," said the father anxiously, "you don't understand. It will mean that we will have to give up our house and all the beautiful things you have gathered through the years; rugs and jewels and pictures—"

"Of course!" said Mother nonchalantly. "Why speak about such trifles. We've been poor before. Besides, don't you remember what the minister said on Sunday, that we must thank God for the hard things that come into our lives as well as for the nice things? There's probably some wise reason in all this, and maybe by and by we'll see it. Come on, now, let's go to dinner. It's waited long enough. And it's a good dinner, beefsteak and mushrooms. If we're not going to be able to afford such things any more we can at least enjoy this one; unless, Christopher, you think we ought to give this dinner to some creditor?" she asked with a twinkle.

Christopher senior took his wife in a tender embrace and smiled, his whole anxious face relaxing, and Chris Junior murmured as he turned away to brush aside a strange blurring that came into his eyes: "Gosh, Mother, you're a whiz! Who'd ever think you'd take it like that?"

"But I'm getting old, Mother," said the banker wistfully. "It's not as if I could begin all over again."

"So am I," said Mother cheerfully, "But Chris is young, and an old head and a young head together are more than twice as good as just a young head making young mistakes. Come, hurry and carve that steak!"

And surprisingly they sat down at that belated dinner laughing.

If the prowler in the shrubbery outside the dining room window heard that laughter it perhaps only added fuel to the fire in his heart, his angry heart that wanted his money, wanted it to-night, and meant to get it somehow soon.

It was not until Chris got up to his own room a couple of hours later, for they had lingered talking it out and clinging together for reassurance, that he suddenly realized what this change of circumstances was going to mean to him. On the bed lay a pennant in flaming colors bearing the name of his college. He had bought it to-day to give to Gilda to put on her wall, and now he was not going back to college!

He was filled with the consternation of this fact as he finally put out his light and opened his window, and he failed to see the lurking figure with the menacing white face that lurked in the hedge beyond the rhododendrons. He got into his bed and began to look his misfortunes in the face and it was not till those still deep dark hours toward morning that he fell into a light sleep.

And then, suddenly, a shot rang out, almost in the room and he sprang out of bed in alarm!

3

WHEN Natalie Halsey entered the house after watching Chris drive off, she tiptoed softly down the little dark hall and cautiously opened the door into the kitchen to lay down her bundles on the kitchen table. Then she peered through the half open door into the front room which had been temporarily converted into a bedroom during her mother's sickness. The house boasted of but four rooms, two upstairs and two down, with a little lean to shed for a laundry.

"Yes?" said a quick alert voice from the shadows of the sick room, and Natalie threw the door open wide and gave a gay little laugh.

"I can't move without your hearing me, can I, Mother dear!" she said coming in and pushing up the shades at the window to let the brightness of the day in. "I hoped you would have a good long sleep while I was gone. You scarcely slept a wink all night, and you simply have to make it up you know or you'll have a relapse. Didn't you even get a nap at all this morning?"

"Oh yes," said the invalid indifferently, "I think I did, but I kept one ear open for your coming." She gave a funny, brave little laugh as if it were not a matter of importance. "I'm really not tired you know. I'm quite rested. And I've decided to get up to-day and go to work. I've got to finish that hemstitching for Mrs. Baker."

"Now, Mother, look here! You've got to behave!" said Natalie firmly. "You're not getting up until the doctor says so, and not even then unless you are good. As for that old hemstitching, I may as well tell you that Janice finished it weeks ago, and took it to Mrs. Baker, and she was wonderfully pleased with it and paid for it right away. So you don't need to think of work yet awhile."

The mother gave her a startled look.

"The dear child!" she said tenderly. "Was that what she was doing so quietly when I was supposed to be asleep? And I thought she was studying."

"Oh, she studied too," said Natalie gaily.

"But—" the mother's eyes had a worried look. "The money must be all gone. I can't see how you have kept things up—and gotten me luxuries too. I know you two have just starved yourselves."

"Do we look starved?" chirped Natalie cheerily. "Mother, you just quit worrying and I'll tell you some good news. Listen. I've got a job! Not just a little snatch of work, but a real job with a regular salary and hours. I start in Monday morning at 8 o'clock sharp! Now, will you be good?"

"Oh, Natalie! Child! Where is it?"

"Well, maybe you won't like it so well, but it's really good pay, and easy hours, and quite respectable and nice. Just think how wonderful it will be not to have to worry from one six months to another. And then not know whether the dividend we ought to get from our one-and-only is really coming or not."

"Tell me, dear! What is it?"

"Well, it's cashier in the chain store. Now, Mother, don't look that way. It's a really lovely store, clean and light and airy, and the nicest courteous manager. He treats me like a queen. He's having my little glass den all painted up new for me and getting me a stool that will be comfortable. He's married, and kind, and he says his wife told him that it made all the difference in the world what kind of a stool the cashier had, whether she got tired and cross or not."

Mrs. Halsey made a little sound like a moan.

"Oh, Natalie, my baby! To think of your having to work in a store with a lot of rough men! Oh, how badly your father would feel if he knew we had come to that! He was so particular about his dear girls."

"Nonsense! Mother!" said Natalie a trifle sharply because of the sudden lump that came in her throat, and threatened tears. "Father would be glad I had the chance of such a nice place. They are not rough men, any of them. They are just nice pleasant boys that work so hard they haven't time to look at anybody. It's mostly ladies that I'll have to do with. People who come shopping. I'll be sort of shut away in a little glass room you know and people come to the window with their checks and money. I think it'll be fun, Mother. You know I always could make change accurately, and anyway there's a machine to do it. It will be just nothing but fun."

"You're a brave little girl," said her mother wiping away a few weak tears with a feeble hand.

"There, now, Mother dear, just stop those sob-tears this minute. This is nothing to be sad about. Just be glad. Why, Mother I thought you taught me that God takes care of us and nothing that He does not allow can come to people who are His own. Don't you think he can take care of me as well in a chain store as in a fine parlor?"

"Oh, yes," sighed the sick woman. "Of course, but—"

"But it's not the way you would like it done? Is that it, Mothie? Well, say! Don't you think He loves me as much as you do? Come, Mother dear. Cheer up. We're on the road to wealth. Can't you rejoice with me?"

"Oh, yes," said the mother fetching a watery little smile. "You're a good girl."

"No, I'm not particularly good. Don't make the mistake of overestimating my worth," said Natalie comically. "I'm quite natural and normal as a human girl. I envied Gilda Carson this morning. She was out with a great lovely hound on a chain, only I wouldn't keep mine on a chain if I had him. I'd teach him to run alongside and never stray away, or bark at other dogs. Say, Mothie, you don't know how I came home just now, do you? Did you happen to hear me arrive? I just came home in a wonderful new car, with a perfectly good handsome young man. I wish you had been at the window just to see how fine I was. He asked me to take a ride too, only I knew I had to get the soup on for dinner so I declined."

"A young man?" said the mother fearfully, "Oh, Natalie, *who?*"

"Oh, you needn't sigh like that, Mother. He was perfectly all right. He has the name of being as good as he is good looking. It wasn't a tramp nor a drummer, nor anybody wild from down on the Flats, it was the son of the president of our bank if you please. Christopher Walton, with a span new car that his father has given him to take back to college."

"Natalie! How did he happen to ask you?"

"Oh, he just rode alongside the sidewalk and asked me if he could give me a lift. You know I had some groceries, and I suppose I may have looked overburdened," said Natalie taking half the joy out of her unexpected ride, by this flat facing of facts. "He's always been noted for his kindliness."

"That was—*nice* of him," said the mother thoughtfully. "That's the kind of young man that you might naturally have had for a friend if all things had gone well with us and your father had lived. Of course he wouldn't think so now, though. He wouldn't know from present appearances that your father was just as good as his."

"Oh, Mother, don't talk that way!" said Natalie with a sudden brief impatience. "We all had Adam for a remote grandfather, anyway. What's the difference about family?"

"Because,—dear child, you don't understand. But class really means a lot to most people. It probably does to him. Most young men in his station in life would only look upon one in your position as someone to condescend to."

Natalie was silent for a moment.

"Well, suppose he did?" she said with matter-of-factness in her tone. "I had a nice ride anyway, and he talked to me just as if I was any nice girl. He used to be in my class in High School you know. It really wasn't anything so very notable, just a few blocks in a pretty car, but it was fun and I'm glad I had it."

"Yes, of course," the mother hastened with belated pleasure to state, "so am I. How I wish you had a car of your own."

"Oh, now Mother, what would we do with a car of our own here in this street? Where would we keep it? On the front porch or out in the little old forsaken chicken coop?"

At last Natalie got her mother to laughing a little. Then she suddenly sobered.

"Dear child!" she said with a quiver in her voice.

"There's something else about this that makes me troubled. I wouldn't want you to get interested in a handsome young man who might offer you a ride now and then, and mean nothing by it, and then break your heart."

Natalie sat down in the rocking chair and broke out laughing, perhaps to help her hold back the tears which were very near the surface this morning, for in spite of her brave words and cheery manner, things were looking pretty serious for her. She didn't mean to tell her mother that there were only thirty-seven cents of the hemstitching money left after she had purchased the supply of necessities she had just brought home, and that they had had to ask the landlord to let the rent run along until her first week's pay came in before he might expect an instalment on it. Poor child! She had been up and down several times in the night trying to soothe her mother to sleep, rubbing her back with steady patient hand, bathing her aching forehead with witch hazel, getting her a glass of milk, and the strain was beginning to tell on her. To tell the truth it had been a bit hard to contrast the difference between her own life and that of some of the members of her class whom she had seen in brief glimpses as she passed them on the street that morning, and her brave spirit had faltered several times.

So now, she laughed to hide her tears, and put on a gay little comical manner.

"Oh, Mother dear! What a little silly fraid-cat you are! Do you take me for an absolute fool? Don't you know I have no intention of falling for any boy, no matter how fine or how plain he may be. I'm going to hold Mother's hand and stay at home and make life happy for you. Perhaps Janice will marry, and when I get old I'll make bibs and dress dolls for her children, but I'm just cut out for a grand old maid. I'm not going to break my heart for anybody. Now! Will you be good? It's time for your beef tea, and if you find any more causes to worry I'm going to send for the doctor! So there!"

So with coaxing and wiles she cheered her mother to a real smile, and fed her beef tea, and chattered on about how she was going to make over her old green serge for a school dress for Janice, till the day settled into a quiet peaceable groove of homely little duties.

Then Janice breezed in with the announcement that she had an order for a dozen handkerchiefs and three pairs of pillowcases to hemstitch, and the sun shone in the tiny parlor bedroom.

Later when the mother was taking an afternoon nap and the sisters were doing up the brief kitchen work and having a cheery confabulation together about how they were going to make both ends meet, Natalie confided to her sister the story of her ride, and her mother's fears.

"Mums is afraid I'm going to lose my heart at once, of course," she laughed.

"Well," said Janice thoughtfully, "I shouldn't think it would be a hard thing to do, Natty. I think he's perfectly grand. There isn't a single one of your class in High School that's as good looking as he is, nor as polite and really courteous. And he's smart too."

"Oh, sure!" agreed Natalie out of a heart that had held those same opinions through four long lonely years in High School, and three hard-working empty ones since. "That goes without saying. Why look lower than the best. That's why I'm getting ready to be a cheerful spinster. I couldn't possibly aim for the highest, so why aim at all? Oh, Jan! For pity's sake, let's talk about something practical. Do you realize that I've got a job, and that if we can get through till next Saturday I'll have a pay envelope? But how to get through till then is the problem. Suppose you take account of stock. Can we do it? There's still thirty-seven cents in the treasury but Mother's wee dividend doesn't come in for another six weeks yet. How about it? Could we live on beans for a day or two and leave the thirty-seven cents for mother's extras? We can charge beef for beef tea for a week if it comes to a pinch."

"Sure we can," said Janice gallantly. "I've got two pounds of rice, a box of gelatine, half a pound of sugar and some junket tablets hidden away in case of emergency, and there's still a quarter in my once-fat-pocketbook. We'll manage to rub along. With all this you brought in to-day we'll live like kings. That meat will make a wonderful soup, and we'll eat the meat too, and then sandwiches and hash! Oh, sure! And you got a stalk of celery. You extravagant thing! That'll just put pep into any meal."

"He threw that in," said Natalie laughing.

"Oh, *he* did!" said Janice looking at her sister sharply. "Another Red Skin has bit the dust has he? Well, I guess Mother'll have something else to worry about. Which is it to be, Natty, a bank president or a groceryman, that I'm going to have for my best brother-in-law?"

"Oh, stop your nonsense!" said Natalie good naturedly. "Come on and let's clean this cupboard shelf, and find out just to a grain how much of everything we really have left. I shouldn't wonder if by next week Mother will be able to be up a little while each day, and perhaps the next week you could go back to school. Then we'll have to work out a regular schedule of home work, so you won't have too much on your hands while I'm in the store."

So they scrubbed the cupboard shelves, and set their meager array of eatables out grandly, apportioning them for each day of the week, jubilant that it was going to be possible to get through to the first pay day.

"A shredded wheat biscuit apiece, six days," counted Natalie, "not counting to-morrow. We have oatmeal enough left for to-morrow morning."

"His sister is very nice too," mused Janice measuring out the rice carefully and putting it in a clean glass jar.

"What?" said Natalie whirling around upon her sister. *"Whose* sister?"

"Chris Walton's sister," said Janice, her eyes on a tiny bag of raisins that suggested a possible rice pudding if an egg and a little milk could be spared. "We could have rice pudding for Mother's birthday," went on Janice thoughtfully. "She could eat that surely. You know Friday is her birthday. We really ought to have some chicken broth. How about my going out and making a raid on our neighbor's hencoop?"

"Is she indeed?" said Natalie. "What's her name? How do you happen to know that she's nice?"

"Who? The hen I'm going to raid? Now how could I possibly tell what her name is till I've met her?" said Janice in an aggrieved tone.

"I was speaking of the bank president's daughter," said Natalie in a dignified tone, "but if you wish to be trivial it doesn't matter. What's a stolen hen among friends?"

"Why," said Janice giggling, "she's in my class in school and her name's Elise. I think she's nice because she never has any runs in her stockings and she doesn't use lipstick. We don't have much to do with each other of course, how could we? She has her own friends. But she smiled at me the other day when we passed in class. I like her. I think you can usually tell, don't you? Even if you don't know people very well. She never makes me feel the darkened-up runs in *my* stockings the way Gilda Carson does, nor how much too short my old blue dress is getting, and—anyhow, I like her."

"Well, that's nice," said Natalie irrelevantly. "So do I,

if she smiled at you," and she suddenly bestowed a resounding smack on the round curve of her sister's cheek.

"How about stewing these eight prunes?" said Janice, rubbing off her sister's kiss with a grin. "Maybe Mother would like a taste, and they really have been here a long time. Not that I like them," she finished with a grimace. "When you get to be a bank-presidentess, or a lady grocer, whichever it is, please don't let's have prunes any more. I'm ashamed to look a prune in the face I've hated so many of them."

"No, my dear, we'll never have another prune when I attain either of those great estates. We'll have grape fruit served in cracked ice, or honeydew melon with lemon juice, or black grapes from South Africa, just on one provision however, and that is that you cut out that nonsense and never speak of it again. Even in fun I don't like it, Jan," she added seriously. "If I should ever meet Chris Walton again I should be ashamed to think we had ever talked such utter nonsense. Promise me, dear, you won't!"

"You dear old funny serious darling!" said the younger sister in a burst of admiration. "Of course not, if you don't want me to. I was only kidding anyway. But seriously, Nat, I do wish you had some nice friends like that, and some good times like other girls."

"I have all the good times I want," said Natalie with a firm shutting of her lips. "Haven't I the chance to go to Bible School? You don't know how glad I am of that. I've wanted it ever since that first time I went. I'm so glad it doesn't cost anything. I just love every minute of the hour. You are sure you don't mind giving up Monday evenings?"

"Why should I mind, dearest dear? Where would I go? To the opera or to Gilda Carson's dance at the

Country Club, or did you suppose a host of boy friends were waiting outside the door to bear me to the Movies or some other place of entertainment? No, rest your conscience, serious sister, I'll only be falling asleep over my hemstitching or stealing an hour at a hoarded magazine story."

"Oh, Jan, I wish you had some good times! I mean you shall, too, when I get on a little farther."

"Oh, certainly, we'll all have good times," chanted Janice waving the dish towel. "Now, if you don't mind I'll retire to my hemstitching and earn a few honest pennies for a rainy day without prunes."

Softly laughing the two girls scurried upstairs to get their sewing, walking quietly lest they awaken their mother. They had good times together, these two girls who were so almost isolated from their own kind. They were perhaps closer to one another than most sisters just because hard work and poverty had separated them from the girls who would have been their natural mates if their father's fortune had not been swept away when they were very young, and sickness and death had not changed their environment. They chatted quietly as they worked, talking over all the people they had met, all the little trifles that went to make up their days. Natalie asking questions about Janice's school friends, recalling incidents of their older brothers and sisters; and Janice curious about the chain store and her sister's new environment.

At last Janice folded away her hemstitching.

"It's getting too dark for you to work on that green serge any longer, Natalie," she said, "and I can't see to pull the threads. We can't afford to get glasses so we better stop. What's for supper? I'm hungry as a bear."

"Toast and tea and a cup of junket for Mother," said Natalie folding the breadths of the skirt she had just succeeded in cleverly piecing so it wouldn't show. "There's codfish enough left for you and me," she added firmly, "creamed codfish on toast with a dish of dried apple sauce apiece, and warmed over cocoa. We simply have got to hoard every crumb till next Saturday. Can you stand it, Jan?" she looked at her sister anxiously.

"Sure thing," said Janice bravely, almost blithely. "Aren't I husky enough to survive a week of codfish and apple sauce? I might even give up the apple sauce if you'd ask me, especially the dried part. I'm not particularly partial to dried apples. But of course they're not nearly as scratchy to the tongue as dried peaches. I abominate *them.*"

"We're eating the codfish to-night so we can have a meat ball apiece to-morrow," appeased the sister.

"Noble sacrifice!" giggled Janice, "'On to the codfish! Let joy be unconfined! No sleep till morn while youth and beauty meet—' is that the way it goes?"

"Stop your nonsense!" said Natalie smiling. "You'll wake Mother."

"Mother is awake. I heard her stirring as I came by the door. I'm going to light her lamp now. Is her toast ready?"

So they presently gathered about the mother with a tempting tray, tempting as to the delicacy of its preparation if not filled with rare food, and the three of them settled down to cheer one another, a gay, brave little trio, trusting God and upholding one another in all the bright tender ways at their command.

4

THE sound of a falling body below stairs brought Chris swiftly to his senses. He sprang into action, but even so his mother was there before him. He found her kneeling at the foot of the stairs, stooping over his father who lay huddled there with blood upon the floor beside him and blood on the breast of his bath robe.

"Call Doctor Mercer!" she said in a low strained voice, and Chris hurried to the telephone, his heart beating wildly. What had happened? Was his father shot through the heart? Oh, God, what had happened? He thought he should always see that picture of his mother in her delicate blue robe kneeling beside his stricken father, her soft gray curls falling over her slender shoulders, and that look of bravery in her eyes. How pretty his mother must have been when she was a girl! That was a strange thought to come at such an awful time, yet it flung itself at him as he lifted down the receiver.

He was back to the hall in an instant.

"He's on the way," he said soothingly. "Can't I lift him up?"

"No, we'll wait till the doctor comes. Get a glass of water!"

He sprang for the water, noting as he passed the dining room window that it was pushed halfway up from the bottom.

"What was Dad doing down here?" he whispered as he brought the water.

"He heard a noise and came down to investigate," murmured the mother. "I tried to make him wait and telephone for the police but he wouldn't."

Then there was a sound at the door. The doctor had arrived, with a policeman just behind him wanting to know what had happened. The next half hour was a confusion of horror to Chris. Policemen coming and going silently, low murmured directions, fingerprints on the window sill, footprints outside the window; a quick low gasp of pain from the stricken man as he came back to consciousness under the doctor's ministrations; anxious waiting during the search for the bullet which had entered somewhere around the lungs; bandages; subtle pungent odors filling the house; the swift arrival of a trained nurse from the hospital; a bed brought downstairs and his father moved to it. It all seemed like one awful nightmare that could not be true. His father! And yesterday everything had been so wonderful and he had been so thankful that there was nothing dreadful in his life!

Strange that that queer unnatural sermon of Sunday should come back to him now; that one sentence, rather, from the sermon, that he had heard above the joyful reverberation of his thoughts; that suggestion that men ought to be thankful for the hard things that came to them. Bosh! How could they? That was ridiculous! What possible good could come from an experience like this one? How could one believe that terrible experiences were sent in love to any one?

Things settled down into quiet at last. That fearful probing for the bullet was over. It had been found in a gravely serious spot close to the lung. His father lay sleeping under opiates with the white-capped nurse in charge, and silence reigning. The mother was going about with white face and bright brave eyes, getting ready in the kitchen something that the doctor had ordered.

"It's a very serious situation," the doctor told Chris plainly, "but if all goes well he has an even chance of pulling through. You'll have to be a man and take the burden from your mother, son."

Chris with heavy heart straightened his strong young shoulders and bowed gravely. He felt as if the burdens of the universe had suddenly settled down upon him. He felt as if the ground under him was sinking away and everything that he had ever known and trusted in was swimming, toppling about him. But he bowed the doctor out, took all his directions, went and helped the nurse arrange a curtain to keep the light from her patient's eyes, helped his mother in the kitchen, and then persuaded her to lie down and save her strength for later when she might be needed. And at last he was free to go to his own room and change his bathrobe and slippers for more suitable clothing.

He stood in the middle of his room and looked about him dazed. Looked at his watch and stared about again. Was it only three short hours since he had heard that shot? Why, ordinarily at this hour he would still be in his bed sleeping. It was only six o'clock in the morning, yet that house had seemingly passed through a whole day's work!

Was it only yesterday morning he had been so happy

getting his things in shape for packing? There on his desk lay a pile of letters he had sorted out to burn. And there were the piles of new undergarments his mother had marked yesterday and laid on the window seat for him to put in his trunk. College! He couldn't go now of course. And that car? Where was it? He ought to hunt up the police and find out what they did with it. He hadn't thought of it since.

Softly he tiptoed down to the telephone booth in the back hall, and finally got in touch with the police station. They assured him the car was safe, what was left of it, and his heart sank. His next duty would be to communicate with the owner. Would he be liable for the damage or would the insurance cover it? He knew very little about insurance rules. A five thousand dollar car, its beautiful glitter defaced! Another five thousand dollars to add to the hundreds of thousands, perhaps, that his father owed. Well, he would look after that anyway. Somehow he would find a job. He must! He must be a man now and take cares upon himself. Maybe his father would never recover. Even if he lived he might be always an invalid after this. There was that possibility to face.

Yesterday he was facing another happy year of college life, football, basketball, baseball, fraternities, honors, all that college life meant. To-day he might as well be an old man and be done with it. He had debts and a family dependent on him. He dropped his head down wearily on the telephone stand and sighed. If he had not been ashamed he would have cried. He could feel the tears in his eyes and down in his throat. He swallowed hard, and fought them back. He was a man. He had to be! And Dad, his perfectly wonderful dad, was lying in the living room between life and death. Dad might not get well. What did it matter whether he went to college or not?

If Dad ever got well he wouldn't care whether he owned a sport car or not.

Presently he roused himself enough to telephone the agency of the car, ask anxious questions about insurance, and disclose the whereabouts of the car. He was gratefully relieved when they said they would take care of it and let him know later about the insurance. He left the telephone with a sigh, tiptoed to the door of the living room and looked wistfully in. The nurse came and spoke to him in a noiseless voice, telling him to go to bed and snatch some sleep. Chris dragged himself upstairs and threw himself across his bed. The sun was high and bright flinging its rays half across the room but he did not notice it. He was too utterly weary in soul and body, and dropped asleep as soon as his head touched the pillow.

There followed long days and anxious nights when the affairs of the world were practically forgotten in the more vital question of whether the husband and father were going to live or die, and Chris felt that he was aging a year an hour. College was a thing of the past, and he stuffed away all the pennants and athletic articles in a dark closet and tried to forget there was such a thing as being a boy with a care-free life. Yet there wasn't much to actually do. Hang around the halls, listen for the slightest sound from the sick room, go on the trivial errands for nurse or doctor, sometimes in a wild hurry with the helpless feeling that the beloved father's life was slipping away no matter what they did. Once he had to go to the train to meet a famous specialist who was coming in consultation. That was a terrible day that seemed ages long.

As Chris looked back to the afternoon when he and his father had stepped out of the bank door and stood together before that angry mob it seemed years past. Yet he was sometimes conscious of a thrill of pride in his father. If Dad had to go out of life he was glad he had this last brave act to remember. Sometimes when he closed his eyes to try and sleep he could see the noble unafraid look on his father's face as he opened his lips to speak, and stood there so controlled and quiet when the mud was thrown in his face. At such times his blood would boil over the indignity till it seemed he just must get up and go out and hunt for the criminal who did it and throttle him. Then he would get up and begin to pace back and forth in his room like a caged lion, till remembering his father downstairs who might hear, he would force himself to lie down again.

Affairs at the bank seemed a distant and vague interest. Every day someone would call up and ask after the president, and give some hint of how matters were going. Chris knew that a bulletin had been sent out to depositors giving them hope of an instalment in the near future. He knew that his mother had signed over all properties in her name, or in a joint account. He knew vaguely that other directors had done the same, and that there was hope of putting the bank back some day on some kind of a working foundation. But he seemed to have drifted so far away from it all that it did not interest him. His heart seemed frozen, deadened. His universe had turned to stone. He wondered sometimes idly why God could let a catastrophe like this come to his father and mother, such wonderful Christians. And himself! He had never done anything so very bad that he should have to be treated like this. It almost looked as if his father and mother had put their trust vainly in a God.

One day on the street Chris was hurrying along with medicine for which the nurse had sent him, and a man, passing, looked keenly into his eyes with a pleasant glance. The lean, kindly face was vaguely familiar. Somehow battling in his mind against that kindly glance was a former impression of startled antagonism. He glanced back after the man and suddenly it came to him that this was the man who had preached that sermon about being thankful for the hard things as well as the pleasant things that came into one's life. Chris stabbed him in the back with a black scowl and passed on.

"Good guy that is! Knows a lot about it, he does!" he meditated. "Like ta lose all he's got, wouldn't he? Like ta have his father dishonored and shot and lying between life and death for weeks. Like ta give up his chance of getting anywhere in the world because he couldn't finish his college education. You bet he'd be thankful for all that handed out ta him in one day, wouldn't he?"

Chris swung belligerently into his own door and shut it behind him, yet he could not shut out the memory of that kindly glance.

There remained with him an impression of deeply graven lines of sorrow, though the man did not look old.

Gradually as the days passed the tension in the sick room let up a little. The burden on their hearts was not quite so heavy. The father seemed to be improving just a little and hope sprang up fearsomely.

Then, one morning, there came a telephone call from Walter Gillespie's sister. Walter was coming home for a few hours and wanted to see him very much. Could he take lunch with him? He wanted to consult him about something.

Chris was whistling softly under his breath as he got ready. It was good to have the cloud lifted, even briefly, to feel that things were not quite so hopeless in the sick room as they had been, and that he might go out for a few hours without that dread feeling clutching at his heart that death might have entered during his absence. It was good to see Walt again, even though he had been gone from home but a short time. It gave him a warm pleasant feeling to know that Walt wanted to see him, a thrill to think of hearing how things were going at college. It was a salve for his hurt pride that even though he was not coming back to college they valued his opinion enough to want to consult him about something.

As he walked down the street he began to wonder what it could be that Walt wanted. Probably to discuss some questionable men who were up for consideration by the fraternity. It might be Dick Bradford. If so he was absolutely against him. He was yellow. You couldn't depend on him.

As he approached the Gillespie home he suddenly realized that he was on foot instead of driving the handsome new car that he had talked with Walt so much about when he was thinking of getting it. It may have been this thought which obsessed him as he went up the steps, or was it possible that Walt as he came down the stairs and met him in the hall had just the slightest shade of kindly condescension about him as he greeted him? He must be mistaken of course. Walt was never that way with him. With anybody. Walt and he had been buddies since they were little kids. No, of course, he was just sensitive.

Yet he felt it again up in Walt's room, when they were going over the history of the last few weeks in college, Walt telling about the new boys, the prospects of the fraternity, the changes in the faculty. Especially what was being done in the fraternity. Walt had been made president! A sudden pang shot through Chris. There had been strong hints that he himself was to be made president this semester. Then he generously arose to the occasion and put out a cordial hand for the old time grasp!

"Congratulations, Pard!" he said eagerly, his ready smile beaming forth. "That's great!"

Walt accepted his eagerness a bit languidly as befitted one in a higher position and went on to tell of the men that had been pledged.

With studied casualness Walt announced:

"And oh, yes, we're taking in Dick Bradford. That'll be a help."

Chris froze at once. Dick Bradford! Walt knew what he thought of Dick Bradford. Then Walt hadn't come to consult him about that. It was all settled. Chris felt strongly the condescension in his former comrade's manner and he closed his lips quickly in a firm line and then opened them to say with decision:

"You'll be making a great mistake, Walt. He's yellow. I thought I told you what happened last spring—"

But Walt waved him aside.

"He's got personality, Chris. There isn't a man in the new bunch that can match him for that, and we need men with personality, outstanding men, that can represent us anywhere and make a good impression. We feel that we have done a good thing in securing him. In fact we almost lost him to the Deltas. They had him all but pledged."

"He's a typical Delta," said Chris with his old haughty manner that used to bring Walt to terms in the old days. But Walt simply lifted his chin a shade higher and smiled superciliously.

"You always did have it in for Dick," he said condescendingly, "but your advice is a bit late. Dick was pledged last night, and we feel that he's the right man. He has charm you know. And now, Kid—"

Chris frowned with a sudden quick chill at his heart. This wasn't the old kindly "Kid" of his childhood, it was a condescending tone, a term of diminution. It was as if they had suddenly changed places and the admiring deference which Walt had always paid him, had suddenly been demanded of him. Did it do this to Walt to become president of the fraternity for a semester? Would it have done that to himself?

But Walt was talking fluently now.

"We had a get-together last night, some of us who are in at the heart of things, and decided that it wasn't fair to your college to have a man like you drop out just at the end this way."

He spoke as if Chris had dropped out through sheer wantonness. Chris looked up at him in astonishment.

"We feel that it is due the college and our class that you should finish. You had a fine record all the way through, both athletics and studies, and neither the class nor the teams can afford to lose you at this stage of things. We feel you should come back and finish."

Chris lifted his chin and looked at his old comrade coldly. This was not even the old tone of sympathy and love that he felt he had a right to expect from Walt. He was talking as if he were an officer who had a right to rebuke him.

"In short," went on Walt putting on a grown-up official manner, "we felt that something should be done for you. So we have looked around and found several ways of helping out. With an athletic scholarship we can fix things so that you will have practically nothing to pay. Of course you wouldn't be able to occupy the suite that we had expected to take together," Walt's eyes were on the floor now, fitting the toe of his well polished shoe into the pattern of the oriental rug. "You wouldn't expect that. And anyhow, Dick has taken over your share in the apartment so that would be impossible even if you could afford it, but there is a room vacant on the fourth floor and I think you could be fairly comfortable there. Of course it's among the freshies but that would be a part of the concession I believe from the college, some duties up there—"

He paused suddenly and looked up, worried by the stony silence with which Chris was receiving his offer.

Chris was sitting there with his haughtiest manner, his head thrown up, his eyes angry, looking at his friend as if he had suddenly become an alien enemy.

Walt began to fidget around uneasily. He knew that look on Chris's face but had never happened to have it turned on him before. He hastened to speak in quite a different tone.

"Why, what's the matter, old man? You don't understand. I'm offering you a chance to finish your college course. I've come down on purpose. The Frat sent me. They're back of me, and they'll be back of you. And the college wants you."

"Sorry!" said Chris stiffly. "It's quite impossible."

"But look here, Chris," said Walt getting nervous. He had thought this thing was going to be put through so easily. "You don't understand. It won't cost you a cent. It's a free gift! The college feels you're worth it to them! They haven't a man who can come up to you in athletics, and they really need you."

"That's gratifying, I'm sure," said Chris assuming his most grown-up manner, and shutting his lips with that kind of finality that made his former playmate remember other occasions, and understand that this was going to be a real hand-to-hand battle.

He settled down to argue. He still had several good reasons to give why Chris should come back with him to-day to college.

"Why, I've had this ready to propose for a week, but I wouldn't do it until your father was out of danger," he said in a conciliatory tone that helped a lot toward soothing Chris's wounded pride.

"My father isn't entirely out of danger yet," said Chris in a serious tone. "He's better, but we have to take very great care of him."

"Oh, certainly! Of course!" said the other young man a trifle impatiently. "But a nurse can do that! He would get well twice as quick if he knew you were back in college getting all that's coming to you. Why, I've had my sister on the qui vive watching the bulletins from the doctor and she wired me the minute he said your father was better."

"That wouldn't make any difference," said Chris, and suddenly knew he was right. "It will be a long time before my father is well, and I'm needed right here. I have responsibilities. And you're mistaken about Dad. I'm sure just now under the existing circumstances that Dad would expect me to stand by."

But Walter Gillespie did not give up. He argued it this way and that. It presently appeared that another member of the fraternity had come down with him, an alumnus, was to be there to lunch, and Chris had it all to go over again.

But Chris did not weaken. As the argument went on he only grew stronger in the knowledge of what he had to do. A vision of that angry mob in front of the bank the day as he stood by his father and promised to see that his covenant with the people was made good, came vividly to his mind, and convinced him that unquestionably his place was here at home helping his father to make good, cheering and helping his mother.

Later, when he was by himself, all the tempting things they offered would come back to him and stab him to the heart with longing to go. For before they were done with him the jobs they had secured for him, the fourth story dormitory, and the condescension were scrapped, and the beautiful suite of rooms with Walt for room mate was even offered free, with the promise to put Dick Bradford elsewhere. There was a satisfaction of course in the thought that they wanted him so badly. It healed his wounded pride when the dignified alumnus even descended from his patronage, and humbled himself to tell Chris that he was the only man they knew who could come in at this time and tide the fraternity over a certain crisis through which it was passing.

But when it was all over Chris could only say it was impossible, that he had other obligations which came first.

Of course on the way home that afternoon, having seen Walt and the alumnus off on the two-fifty train, he suffered a reaction, and began to think perhaps he had been a fool to refuse such an offer. Perhaps his father would blame him for taking things in his own hands this way. Yet there remained, like a wall of adamant, back in his mind, the knowledge that he should stay and work, and help to pay back his father's debt if possible. At least help him in his present need.

A deep gloom settled down upon him as he turned his steps toward home. Here was he with the way open to go back and get his last college year, which any fool would tell him he needed before he would be worth much in the business world; and yet the way so effectually blocked by honor that the offer might as well never have come save for the satisfaction of knowing how the college people felt toward him.

But when he entered the house and found that his father's condition had not been quite so good that day, he forgot all about college again as the mantle of anxiety returned upon his weary young shoulders.

5

THERE came a morning when the doctor came out of the sickroom with a look of bright triumph on his face.

"Well sir," he said to Chris as he got himself into his fall overcoat and took up his hat, "your father's going to get well. I didn't tell you before because I wasn't sure but there might be a set back, he's come through his worst danger now. The lung is all cleared up, and he's on the way to health again. From now on you won't need to keep quite so still when you walk through the hall, and in a few days he'll be up and around. But don't worry him about business, hear? Not till he's strong. Positively not a word. I've told him I won't have it."

But the sick man seemed strangely apathetic about the affairs of the world. Somehow in the dimness of that darkened chamber he had caught a vision of something bigger than earthly things, and he lay back and rested.

One night shortly before Thanksgiving when Chris, just in from the crisp outside air, came as usual to the invalid chair to which the father had been promoted, he looked up and smiled wistfully at his son.

"Sorry, boy, about the college, but—maybe there'll be a way yet," he said sorrowfully.

"Oh, Dad!" cried the boy, summoning a simulated brightness which he did not feel. "Don't you worry about college! I'm all right. Just so you get well, that's all we care."

"Well, you're a good boy!" said the father tenderly, "and please God, I'm going to get well. The doctor promises me that by the fifteenth of December if I'm good I may go down to the bank. So you see I'm really progressing. And son, Mother and I have been talking about this house. We think the sale ought to be put through as soon as possible for the sake of our creditors."

"The doctor said you mustn't talk about business yet," said the boy, feeling as if his father had struck him.

"No, I'm not going to, Chris, only I didn't want you to be utterly unprepared if somebody comes here to look at the house. The doctor said it wouldn't do me any harm. In fact it is a great relief to me to feel that I am doing all in my power to make up to my creditors. You won't mind, Chris."

"Of course not!" said Chris shortly swallowing the lump that had begun to rise in his throat, and the utter rebellion in his heart. He thought bitterly of the deputation that had come from college to say that they had arranged a way in which his last college year could be financed, but he had not even told his mother about it. He knew that he was needed at home for a long time yet, and that even if his father regained his usual health and was not actually physically dependent upon him, that he should stay at home and get a job; stick by and make it as easy for the family as he could. He knew that this was right. But he was feeling just a little proud of himself, and set up too, that he had taken the stand, refusing the offer courteously but definitely, and had kept his mouth entirely shut about it. He felt quite a little bitter at the world, and unconfessedly at God too, for "handing him out such a raw deal," as he phrased it.

But the next day Chris began to look for a job in good earnest. Up to that time he had not felt that he should be away from the house more than a few minutes at a time lest he should be needed.

It is true that Chris had from the beginning felt easy in his mind about job hunting. Of course he knew all about the unemployed situation, and that older men than himself with families dependent upon them were looking vainly for jobs. He knew this in a general way, but still it never entered his head that he would have a hard time hunting something to do, a real paying job. He felt that his father's son would be welcomed as an employee in any one of a dozen big concerns in town. He wasn't expecting to be a bank president right at the first of course, but he did expect that several places would be open to him at a good salary just because he was Christopher Walton junior.

He had carefully looked the situation over, weighing the wisdom of undertaking a position as a bond salesman, as a cashier in a bank, as an assistant in a real estate office looking toward a partnership, or something in insurance. They all appealed to him in various ways. A managership in one of those big oil corporations might be good too. Of course he expected a six month's training in anything before he would be put in a responsible position with a worth while salary.

No, Chris was not conceited as we usually count the meaning of that word. He was simply judging probabilities by his old standards, as his father's son, the son of the leading bank president in town. He had as yet no conception of what it meant to be a bank president whose bank had closed its doors and put hundreds of poor people in destitute situations. A bank president, it is true, who had promised to give up everything and stand by his creditors, but after all a failure. And Chris was yet to find out that even nobility sometimes begets contempt. He even came to the place once where he wondered if some people would not have respected his father more if he had kept his own millions and lived on in his big house, with servants and cars galore. He came to the place where he found that some men respected money more than even honesty, bowed to it, deferred to it, honored those who had it. His young, furious, indignant soul had many things to learn and many experiences to pass through before he found peace.

So Chris started out early the next morning to find his "position" as he called it, expecting to be able to announce his success to his father on his return.

Chris went first to the three best known bond houses in the city, the heads of which were supposedly personal friends of his father. The head of the first was in conference and declined to see him that day. The head of the second was in a hurry and told him so at once, but informed him coolly that there was no opening with their house at present. They were thinking of dismissing a couple of men, rather than taking on any. Perhaps in the spring. How was his father? He glanced at his watch and Chris knew the interview was over.

The third one frankly told him that there was no business at present to warrant taking on new men, and that even if there were, he, Chris should finish college before he thought of applying for such a job. He suggested that money could be borrowed for his last college year, and when Chris indignantly told him he was needed at home and informed him of his invitation to go to college under scholarships, the man shook his head and told him that it was simply crazy to decline that offer, that his father would never allow him to be so foolish when he was well and around again.

There might of course be truth in some of the things the man said, but Chris closed his lips and left. He could not tell this friend of his father's how utterly destitute they were going to be, and how he must work to help his father and mother. He simply closed his lips and left.

All that day he went from place to place, marking each one off his list as he left it, his heart growing heavier and heavier, and more bewildered, as he plodded on. The bright prospects which he had held as many, and to be had for the asking, were receding fast.

His sore heart was not made lighter by meeting Gilda Carson just getting into Bob Tyson's car. She was home from college for the Thanksgiving holiday, and she tossed him the most casual smile, hardly as if she knew him at all. Never an eager lighting of the face, nor a joyous calling out to him to be sure and come over that evening. Just a cool bow, and she was off, smiling up at Bob as they drove away together.

He frowned and walked half a block beyond his destination, telling his bitter heart that he didn't care in the least what Gilda did, nor what Bob Tyson thought nor anything. He didn't care! He didn't care! He didn't care! But yet he knew in his sore heart that he did care. He cared that his pride had been hurt. Gilda herself wasn't worth caring about of course. In a sense he had always known that, but he had enjoyed taking the prettiest girl in school about and getting her away from others whenever he chose. And to have her freeze him out this way just because his father had lost his money! Well, he was off her for life anyway, and he'd show her, he said fiercely to himself.

He thought with a pang of the fellows off in college, the boys he had played baseball with and football. If the fellows were only back home about town it would be different. He wouldn't feel so alone. Boys never high-hatted like girls. If Walt Gillespie were only home now he would show them all a thing or two. Walt was his best friend. Of course Walt had been a bit lofty when he first began to tell about his being president of the fraternity, and that about Dick Bradford, and come to think about it Walt hadn't written since he went back. Of course college life took a lot of time and fellows weren't keen on writing letters. But—well—if it had been Walt who had to stay at home he wouldn't have left him cold without a word that way. He might have found time for a post card. Just some word about the winning of a game or how the frat was going or something.

A new pang shot through him and his bitterness continued to grow.

He came home at night dog-weary, his young face almost haggard, with gray lines about his eyes and mouth. His mother watched him anxiously across the table but asked no questions. She knew, as mothers know, without asking, that he had been out to hunt a job and had not succeeded!

The next morning when he started on his rounds among a less aristocratic group of firms, he had his jaw set firmly. Before night he would find something. He would force himself in somewhere. It was ridiculous that nobody wanted him. There was a place for him some-where. He hadn't tried but one day yet. Of course he would find something before night.

About ten o'clock as he was passing the station he spied Betty Zane descending from the train with her suit case, home for Thanksgiving from her co-educational college.

"Hello, Chris!" she waved to him, "Can't you take me home in your lovely new car?"

There seemed to Chris's sensitive ear, a mocking tone in Betty's voice. Betty Zane knew of course that he had no new car now. She must have been thoroughly informed of all that happened since she went away. If no one else would tell her, her sharp eyed kid sister Gwendolen would have done so. Betty was just trying to make him confess that he had no car. Betty was like that. She used to pin a butterfly to her desk top in school and enjoy watching the poor fluttering wings. Chris hardened his heart, remembering Gilda's freezing bow of yesterday and he gave Betty a very good male imitation of it, and answered quite rudely for a boy who had been brought up to be courteous:

"Nothing doing. I'm out on business. There's the taxi."

Betty stared at him and tossed her head, then turned her back upon him, and Chris moved on out of her sight, all the more out of sorts with the world because he knew that he ought to be ashamed of himself.

So he tramped on, bitter and pessimistic. Grand day this for the day before Thanksgiving!

Oh, of course he was glad and thankful that Dad was getting better and Mother wasn't breaking under the strain. But even that had a sting in it, for what prospect had Dad but bitterness and disappointment? It would be better perhaps if they had all died together rather than to live on and see such a difference between their former life and now. How could they ever be happy again? Dad would probably find that men in the business world could be just as offish as the young folks. Dad wouldn't keep that cheery exalted look long after he got back into business life again. He would find he was up against it. It was all well enough to be so relieved that his good name was to be cleared and no one have to suffer for the bank's troubles, but just wait till the excitement blew over. Dad would suffer. Just suffer! And so would Mother, and it was up to him to do something about it. He'd simply *got* to get a real paying job.

Then he let himself into the house to find that his father and mother were rejoicing, yes, actually rejoicing that the beautiful family car, the car they had had for only about four months, and which had been the delight of their hearts, had been sold at a good price. What did they care how much the old thing brought since they had to give it up?

Father had family prayers as usual, reading a chapter about the goodness of the Lord, and actually thanking God that the car had been so well sold! Well, it was just inexplicable, that was all. For his own part he felt so rebellious at the going of their car that he could hardly make his knees bend to kneel down with them. Thank God for that? There wasn't a chance!

As they rose from their knees after prayer Mr. Walton said with a ring to his voice that his son could not understand:

"I heard to-day of a possible customer for the house. If that be so we may soon be on an honest basis."

"Honest?" burst forth Chris.

"Yes, son," said the father turning wise kind eyes toward him. "I shrink every day from coming out of a house like this when many depositors in the bank that was under my care, people who trusted in me to take care of their all, are almost without food or shelter."

And Chris perceived that his father and mother were bent on but one thing, the paying of their debts, and that possessions meant nothing to them so long as a single creditor had aught against them.

He opened his lips to ask, "But where shall we go, Dad, if the house is sold?" and then was ashamed in the face of such nobility as both parents were displaying, and closed them again.

So, the house was going too! That was another thing to dread! It was like standing on a tiny speck of land in the midst of a wild whirling ocean, and seeing the land crumble away under one's feet bit by bit. The car had gone to-day, college yesterday, the house where he was born would perhaps go to-morrow. And where were all the friends of the years? Would any of them stick, or would they melt away, one by one till they stood alone in an alien world?

6

IT was not until the week after Thanksgiving that the buyer came to look at the house. Chris had almost begun to hope that he was a myth and no one would come.

He was a big pompous man who murdered the King's English and wore an enormous diamond on his fat little finger as if it were a headlight.

He had a large family of untamed children who swarmed gayly, boldly through the house, fingering Mrs. Walton's delicate embroideries, staring into her private room rudely, yelling at one another from one story to another, and even attempting to be what Chris called "fresh" with him, the son of the house.

They freely discussed the furnishings, laughed at some things as funny and old fashioned, were frankly curious about some of the rich tapestries which the Walton's had counted among their finer treasures, asked questions without stint, gaining new viewpoints one could see with every icy answer that Chris made as he showed them over the rooms at his mother's request. As he progressed from cellar to attic, his rage and indignation increased. Why did they have to stand this sort of thing from these low-down, common people? It was bad enough to have them buy the house without this torture. If they wanted it let them take it and keep still. If they didn't let them go away! He had no patience with his mother's smiling sweetness, her gentle courtesy. He knew it was as hard for her as for him. Yet she kept her strength and sweetness. How could she? These insufferable people! They were fairly insulting and acted as if the house belonged to them already. One berouged daughter with too much lipstick said she hoped he would call on her often. It would be nice and cozy having someone come who knew the house well, and he'd likely be homesick and would enjoy coming back. He looked at her coldly and said nothing. He waded deep into the waters of humiliation that day.

It was rumored that the father was a bootlegger and had made an enormous sum of money which he didn't know how to spend. He was voluble in his delight in the house, offered to buy the pictures and hangings and furniture, even the precious works of art that Dad and Mother had picked up abroad. They wanted the house just as quick as the Walton's could possibly get out. They made no question about the price that was asked. They even offered to pay a bonus if they could have possession in two weeks.

Chris, with a curl of disgust on his lip, looked to his father for a quick refusal, but when he saw the relief on that pale, beloved face, and realized that what his father wanted more than anything in life was a speedy release from indebtedness, a quick relief for his depositors, he closed his lips hard on the protest he was about to make. After all of course it was a good price the man was paying, and a bonus would help too. He must remember that they were paupers and had no right to pick and choose.

Oh, those were bitter days for Chris, tramping the streets all day, sometimes far into the evening, sometimes walking miles into the country to reach a man who had influence.

Then came the question of where they would go. Chris faced it bitterly, thinking of lodging houses or boarding houses, or a hotel apartment. But the next night when he came home and heard the plan his mother and father had agreed upon he thought his cup of humiliation was full.

There was a little old run down house on a back street whose kitchen windows looked out upon the railroad, a street where the washerwoman lived. It had recently come into Mr. Walton's hands through the death of a man without family who owed him a debt of long standing and had given him a judgment note against the house. Chris's family were actually planning to move into it the next week and vacate their noble family mansion for the bootlegger's family. Chris sat down in the nearest chair aghast.

Elise was there, having been summoned home from her aunt's where she had been while her father was ill. Elise in her pretty blue dress, with her fair curling hair and her lovely big blue eyes. Somehow she had never looked so lovely before to her brother's eyes as when he thought of her in Sullivan Street living next their washerwoman!

Before he could shut his lips, so carefully guarded during all the weeks when his father lay ill, one awful sentence about Elise and Mother living next the washerwoman slipped out, and Chris saw the dart of pain in his father's eyes at once.

"But," said Elise gayly, "she won't be our washerwoman any more you know, Chrissy, because, as I understand it, we can't afford any washerwoman. We have to do the wash ourselves. I think it'll be fun," she ended with a grin of good sportsmanship.

"I know!" sighed the father with a piteous look around upon them all.

"Nothing of the kind!" said Elise, "Mother and I are going to enjoy it, aren't we, Mother? It'll be the chance of a lifetime for me to learn to be a good cook and housekeeper. Forget it, Daddy! This is only a game. Get into position and smile!"

And her father, in spite of his heavy heart, smiled at the pretty girl.

"Maybe it'll only be for a little while," he murmured, trying to make his voice sound hopeful.

That night Chris bought a paper and spent two hours studying the want advertisements, and marking them. As he finally got into his bed he thought of the fellow who had preached that fool sermon the last time he went to church, and wished he could wring his neck. A lot he could be thankful for the things that were handed out to him now, couldn't he? Mother and Elise in a place like Sullivan Street! Good night! He'd *got* to get a job. Even if it wasn't so high up, he'd got to get a *job!*

He didn't call it a position any more, it was just plain job. He felt he might even be a little thankful if he could just have a few dollars coming in to help out. No creditor was going to get his money, not till he was making enough to put Mother in a comfortable position anyway.

The next morning he started out early and answered three advertisements, but found a long line of discouraged looking applicants waiting for each. While he was waiting for a fourth place which had named a time for applicants to arrive, he stepped around to Sullivan Street, and found it even worse than he had feared.

The house was whitewashed, or had been once, but

there was scarcely enough of the original to identify it. It looked through the dirty windows to have but five rooms and a lean-to kitchen. There were four dirty limp cords fastened from stakes in the hard ground to the top of the front window sash, and twined about them were four dead dried ghosts of morning glory vines waving disconsolately about in the chill November breeze. They typified to Chris their family of four Waltons, come down to Sullivan Street from the glory of the ancestral home which had been theirs.

The dead leaves waved and rasped emptily, back and forth, against the broken window pane making a sad little minor refrain of weird music that sent a lump into the boy's throat. He dashed around the narrow path to the back yard, a mere patch, mostly paved with ashes, and saw a tattered clothes line stretched from the corner of the house to the fence and back, and fancied his beautiful young sister hanging up the family wash thereon in a chilly wind like this. The tears stung into his eyes. He hurried off and tried to forget it all, wishing for a genie and a magic lamp wherewith to bring an immediate fortune for the family. He went on to the next place on his list, was told they wanted only college graduates, and turned with more bitterness in his heart.

Thankful for a thing like this? Not he? Where was his father's God anyway? Hadn't there really been any God at all, he wondered as he buttoned his coat closer, and pulled his hat over his smarting eyes. He had a feeling at the pit of his stomach like to his memory of the day he first discovered there wasn't any real Santa Claus.

What was going to happen next, he wondered desperately, and pulled his hat further down over his eyes.

The next few days were soul-trying ones for Chris beyond anything he had ever experienced before. He was appalled to find that his mother and father were both determined to move to the Sullivan Street house. Even the first desolate glimpse of the house had not discouraged them.

He had watched them as they came in sight, walking, the first time they had been out since the car was sold, walking down the plebian street like common folks. Chris raged inwardly and followed behind them, dropping his eyes, hoping they would not meet anyone who knew them.

"I'm afraid it looks pretty hopeless," sighed the father. "If I just didn't remember what wonders you can work with very simple things I would give up in despair. But we could be happy there for a little while, couldn't we, Mary? Perhaps something will change, and we can get into a better neighborhood soon."

"We can be very happy!" said Mary with a toss of her head and that bright smile she had worn ever since her elderly lover had begun to get well.

"A little paint will work wonders," she said. "We can save on butter and things and buy the paint and Chris and I can put it on. I'll do the inside and Chris will do the outside. There's a pair of nice new overalls that I bought for the chauffeur and never gave to him. They will do for Chris, and we have a ladder, haven't we?"

Whether it was the vision of himself in overalls on a ladder painting that Sullivan Street house, or the rainbow cheerfulness of his mother's voice, one or the other or both brought sudden tears to Chris's eyes and he had to duck his head down quickly and pretend to be trying to pick up a round bit of tin that looked like a dime from the sidewalk, lest his father should see him crying. Tears! In a fellow old enough to be in college! Why, he hadn't felt like crying since he was a baby and licked all the boys in the street, and then found his nose was bleeding and one eye wouldn't open.

Mother hadn't been discouraged with the inside of the house either. She had said how it was good they had never sold that coal range in the cellar at home. Nobody would want to buy that. They were out of date now. But it would practically heat the house in mild weather, and a coal range was wonderful to cook with. You could broil a beefsteak to a perfection over hot coals that would make a gas-broiled steak blush with shame. Cheerily like that she talked along, suggesting that the old red sofa from the attic, the one that had been her mother's and she had never been willing to part with, even though it was shabby and old-fashioned, would fit in between the side windows that looked out on the alley. She recalled also a little old stand, and a queer old pine desk that had been her father's, and a few over-stuffed chairs. It had been mere tender memories that had kept them in the attic instead of sending them to the dump. But now, why! she looked almost glad with that tender touch in her eyes as if she were actually pleased that they were to come into their own again. Her son stood by the dusty window and looked out marveling.

And the very next morning he came home and found his mother washing that dirty window out of which he had looked! He had come home for lunch, and the one maid who was staying with them till they were moved said lunch was ready but his mother had gone down to "the other house." The words gave his heart a wrench. As if that little dump down there could be called a house! "The *other* house!" He had followed hot foot after her, and found her washing windows, her sleeves rolled up, an old sweater pinned around her closely, and a stray lock of the wavy gray hair fallen into her eyes, her face as eager as a child's. The wife of the president of the Fidelity Bank washing windows in late November in a cold house!

He took her home summarily, walking so fast she was almost out of breath, and scolding her all the way, but she only smiled. After that he went back after lunch and finished the rest of the windows himself. He didn't do them very well. They had streaks all over them, but at least the dust was off. Then he looked around in dismay at the work still to be done. Walls, and floors to be swept and washed! Dirty paper, dirty paint! Ugh! How could his mother bear it? It was harder work to wash a window than to play an afternoon's game of football. He was trembling from head to foot. After serious consideration he went home and collected some of his treasures, his camera, several tennis rackets, and a set of golf clubs and took them to a second-hand place and sold them. Then he hunted up a man who did white washing and got him to promise to scrub the whole house early the next morning.

It wasn't very well done. Even Chris's inexperienced eye could see that, as he looked it over the next afternoon, but at least his mother wouldn't have to come into that filthy den, with the grime of no knowing what kind of people on it.

After that Chris abandoned his vain search for a job until the moving should be over. Chris and Elise went to work, Chris with a frown on his handsome face, and Elise with laughter and gay song, jokes, and an indefatigable ability to sit down on the stairs anywhere and giggle at his efforts. Often he got furiously angry at her. He found it impossible to treat this whole catastrophe of the family like a joke. It was serious business, the wreck of their whole lives, and here were Mother and Elise laughing as if they enjoyed it. They were just alike.

Then he would glance at his father, sitting back relaxed, smiling in his invalid chair, not being allowed to lift his finger, and looking very peaceful. What did Dad have that kept him so serene? He was satisfied that Dad was deeply hurt that all these things had to be, cut to the heart that his wife and daughter must work so hard, that his son could not go to college, yet the lines of care were not nearly so deep on his forehead as they had been some weeks before the bank closed its doors. Was it just that he was relieved to be doing his best toward paying the depositors? No it must be something more than that. And in spite of himself he felt a respect for his father's faith. It might have no foundation, but whether it did or not it was beautiful to see such faith. He found a hungry feeling in his own heart to have something like that to stay his furious young heart upon, yet he told himself he never could believe in a God who would do such things to trusting people, and he steadily hardened his heart when he heard his father pray, always beginning his petition with thanksgiving. He simply could not understand it. Elise was only a child of course. She enjoyed every new thing that came along, even moving into a little seven by nine dinky house on a back street, like a child playing doll house. His mother was merely glad that his father was up and around again. Neither Mother nor Elise had any sense of what it was going to mean, this terrible change in the family fortunes! But his father understood, and yet he bore up. It was inexplicable.

Yet somehow in spite of all predictions, when the paint and the paper were in place, and the few old sticks of furniture disposed about, that had been saved from the wholesale carnage, even the old golden oak sideboard and dining table and chairs from the servant's dining room took on an air of comfort. Chris couldn't explain it.

There were draperies too, that Chris remembered in the nursery when he was a kid, gay cretonnes with tie backs, long since packed in an old chest in the attic and

It was that first night that they had supper in the new home.

Elise and her mother in plain cotton dresses were in the speck of a kitchen getting supper and a savory smell was already beginning to pervade the house. The rooms were too near neighbors to have any secrets from the parlor of what was going on in the kitchen. Chris knew that there was one of those savory stews that he always liked so much, and he was hungry for it already. Anna, the departing maid, had cooked it that morning in the old house before the last load of things they were allowing themselves to call their own from the attic came over. Chris knew that Anna had also made dough-nuts and a couple of mince pies on the sly between other duties. He had brought over the stone jar containing the doughnuts and the basket with the mince pies early that morning that Anna's surprise for his mother might be complete. Oh, there would be a good supper.

Elise was setting the table, humming a gay little tune, that never gave hint of the tears that were so near the surface. His father was sitting beside the old attic table in the faded old Morris chair with his feet on the extension, reading the evening paper and resting as happily as if he had been in his gorgeous leather chair in his own library with the carved desk beside him and an alabaster lamp of old world design to light him. Didn't his father know the difference? Didn't he care at all?

And now came a call for Chris to go after a loaf of bread.

"It's only a couple of blocks or so up the avenue, Chris," said Elise cheerfully, as she saw a frown gather on her brother's brow. "I'd go but Mother needs me. Dinner'll be quite ready when you come back. It's one of those chain stores, the second block on the right. I bought a cake of soap there yesterday. You can't miss it."

"Why? Will I see the rest of the box of soap out watching for me?" asked the brother ill-naturedly as he rose and slung his cap on the back of his head, "I thought you got an A in English. Why would the fact that you bought a cake of soap there yesterday keep me from missing the store?"

"Quit your kidding and hurry, please. I'm making popovers and they need to be eaten at once when they're done."

Chris sauntered out into the chilly evening air, perversely refusing to wear his overcoat, and feeling as if he had been exiled into an evil world again. The cheeriness of the little house that had half angered him only made the outside world seem the more unfriendly. How dark Sullivan Street was. The city ought to put in more lights. He hurried along angrily. It seemed to him as if he had scarcely been anything but angry since the bank had closed.

He found the chain store, bright and full of brisk business. Everybody was there inspecting trays of vegetables, buying great creamy slices of cheese, prunes, crackers, coffee, flour and potatoes. One woman had a long list and a pile of groceries on the counter before her, and now she turned toward the meat side of the store and began to select pork chops.

Chris looked around curiously. It was almost the first time since he was a little boy that he had been in such a store. There hadn't been any need. Those things were always well ordered by a capable maid over the telephone. Not even his mother had had to mingle with the common herd this way. The store was bright and cheery.

Everything looked clean and appetizing. There were delightful smells of oranges, celery, coffee, on the air. But no one was paying the slightest attention to him. That gave him a curious sensation. He was used to deference everywhere. Well, of course no one knew him in this section of the city and there was a relief in that. How interested these people were, as if they were selecting a new car or a Christmas present. What did they care which bunch of carrots they bought? Cranberries! How pretty they were in the bulk.

But he must get waited on quickly. He didn't want to stay here all night. He approached a salesman with a lady who was accumulating a great pile of things on the counter. She had come to a pause and was trying to think up something else, gazing up at the top shelves of cereals. He would just cut in on her and get his bread and get out.

But the salesman looked up with a courteous smile.

"Sorry, I'm busy just now. You'll have to wait your turn. Somebody'll be free in a minute I guess."

Chris stepped back haughtily and felt as if he had been slapped in the face. So, there were rules to this chain store game. Everyone was just as good as everyone else. The dark color flung up in his face, and he was about to leave, when he suddenly remembered his recent lowly estate and retreated into the background.

Pinned in a corner by a bunch of brooms and a stack of bargain cans of peaches, watching sullenly for a free salesman, he suddenly heard low spoken words behind him, not meant for his ear he was sure.

"That's him," said an uncultured voice. "He's the old man's only son. Some baby! Yep, right behind ya. Nope, he donno me. I was in Grammar when he was in High. He wouldn't know me from a bag a beans. And anyhow he wouldn't. He always was an awful snob! My goodness, no, I wouldn't speak to him. I wouldn't wantta be high-hatted. I hate snobs!"

Cold angry prickles went down Chris's back, and he felt the very back of his neck grow red. He could hardly come out of his fury when his courteous salesman wheeled upon him at last with a free and easy: "Now, sir, what can I do for you?"

His voice sounded unnatural as he asked for the bread. He didn't remember ever to have bought a loaf of bread before. He wondered if there was a certain way of asking for it. He glowered after the two whispering flappers who had been behind him. They were over at the meat counter now giggling and chewing gum. The one with the red hair and freckles was vaguely familiar as a kid who had once tried to run through a football game in the school yard and made all the fellows furious. She wasn't any account of course, but was that the way all of the school had regarded him, as a snob?

Then his humiliation would be but the greater. They would gloat over his loss of caste. He had never regarded himself as anything but a self-respecting son of his father. A snob was one who looked down on most other people. Well, perhaps he had, but he had always supposed they didn't know it. He had rather regarded it as a breach of etiquette to let others know that they were despised. He must have failed sadly.

He had his loaf of bread at last, and went with the check and his money to the cash window, hastily, to get out before he might meet those two disagreeable flappers, and have to recognize them as fellow buyers.

He handed in his check at the little glass window, and was suddenly aware of a pair of friendly eyes looking up at him and a shyly hesitant smile.

# 7

NATALIE Halsey! Here? Her pale little friendly face seemed like a pleasant oasis in this strange unfriendly environment.

"Hello!" he said, almost eagerly, his face lighting up with a strange relief, "Is this where you hang out? I didn't know it was in this neighborhood."

"Yes," she smiled again, "This is where you picked me up in your new car the other day and took me home. I'll always be grateful to you for getting me home so soon. Mother had had a bad spell just before I left and she was getting very nervous about my being gone so long. She might have had a relapse if I had been much longer."

"You don't say!" he said startled, half pleased to be commended for something he had done after the unpleasant whisper he had just heard behind his back.

"You are home from college for the Thanksgiving holiday, aren't you? Or—that would be over wouldn't it? It must be a week end," she commented in a momentary lull from her store activities.

"No such luck!" he said, a dark cloud of remembrance passing over his face, "I didn't get to college."

"Oh," said Natalie sympathetically, "Someone said you were at home, but I wasn't sure. You—are working somewhere? But you'll enjoy that too. It's nice to be doing something real."

He looked down at the sweet childish face, a little weary, a little blue under the eyes, and felt a sudden tenderness for her, and anger at himself. She was doing something real. She had found it for herself, and he, Chris Walton, couldn't get *anything*. Not *anything!*

"I wish I were," he said wistfully, "I've walked all over this little old town and nobody wants me."

There was a strange humility about his words. Natalie looked up in wonder.

"You don't know of a good job, do you?" he added wistfully.

"Oh," breathed Natalie, her eyes thoughtfully watching him. "Yes, I do. But—you wouldn't want such a job. I'm sure you wouldn't."

"Try me and see," said Chris with sudden determination as he thought of the little cozy room shut in by the cretonne curtains and his beautiful mother in that tiny kitchen getting supper. He must somehow make good. He was desperate.

"But," said Natalie, growing a bit red and confused, "It's only—a—it's not in keeping with your—position," she ended bravely.

"My position, lady," said Chris with a grim humility upon his face that made his chin look rugged and firm, "is away down at the foot of the ladder. I'm groveling at present, if you know what that means. If you have any such jobs as that please lead me to them."

A woman snapped in between them with a five dollar bill to be changed, and two others followed with their checks to be paid, and Chris had to step back for a moment.

He noted Natalie's white fingers as they flew among the dirty bills, checking off dimes and nickels, and wondered that he had never noticed before how delicate and fragile she was. Then the three women moved on and there was another moment's cessation.

"It's only right here, in this store," she eyed him anxiously, "You wouldn't want to work here, would you, in a plain common place like this?"

"I don't know why not," said Chris gamely, swallowing hard at a surprised lump in this throat. "Is there a chance here, do you think? I must get a job."

"We are losing a man to-day," said Natalie. "He got a telegram that his father has died and he must go back to Wisconsin and stay with his mother and get a job there. Our manager is very cross about it. He needs someone right away, but he is very particular. I don't know whether he has found anyone yet or not, and he must have someone Monday. If you could come back at a quarter to nine—we keep open till nine on Saturday nights you know—I could speak to him about it. There might be a chance. But it is only an under position you know."

Some women were approaching loud-voiced among themselves, sticking out checks and money, all talking at once.

"I'll be back," said Chris with sudden determination, and walked away out into the night and the evening smells of the common district where he had come to live. Pork and cabbage, and a fish frying in old grease. Pah! What a neighborhood! And he was going to be a common grocer's clerk, and sell cheese and rat traps and pickled pigs feet to those fat gossipy women! Instead of halfback on the college football team, president of his fraternity, and son of a banker!

He saw himself going around in that crowded store weighing sugar and cutting cheese, and bringing up great cases of cereal and canned stuff. Girls like those two who had pointed him out would think they could say fresh things, and kid with him. How his mother would hate it! How he would hate it!

Yet, there was a kind of elation about him, to think that perhaps there was a job in sight. Besides, hadn't he heard that there was promotion in these stores? Of course he would not stay a common clerk long. If he had inherited any of his father's business ability he could build up and get ahead, and when he got a little money saved up if he didn't like the chain store line he could get into another line. But after all why were not stores where they sold eatables the best thing to tie to? People had to eat no matter how hard the times were, nor what happened. That was an idea, too.

But he wouldn't say anything about it at home until he knew more about it. And then, he hadn't got the job yet, either. Natalie had only promised to speak to the manager. There might be another man by this time, or the manager might think him a snob too. There was no telling in this strange new sad world into which he had come to live, it seemed.

He was almost home before he remembered that he had not thanked Natalie. Little pale-faced, eager, wistful Natalie with her soft halo of hair and her tired trusting eyes. It was kind of Natalie. He had never done anything for her, except to take her home that once with her bundles. Well, he would go back and see, anyway. He wouldn't have it to remember that he had turned any job down, no matter how unsatisfactory.

He came swinging into the house whistling under his

breath forgetting his troubles for the moment. He was thinking that perhaps he was going to get some kind of a break after all. Only a grocery, but something better might turn up later. At least if he could get it he wouldn't be exactly a slacker while he was looking around for something better. Of course the salary wouldn't be large at first while he was learning.

They sat down to dinner as if it were a picnic. Somehow it didn't seem so mournful, after all, as he had expected. Chris thought he would always remember his father's first blessing at the little golden oak table with mother's coarsest table cloth upon it, and the old dishes that had been used mostly in the kitchen at the other house. It was:

"Father, we remember that Thy Son had not where to lay His head at times when He was upon the earth. We thank Thee for this comfortable quiet home that Thou hast given us, and for this evening meal. Make us to show forth Thy glory by the strength of it. Amen."

Chris was very quiet and thoughtful during the meal, jumping up to get a pitcher of water, and replenish the popovers from the pan in the warming oven, to save his mother and sister.

"We have much to be thankful for," said the father looking around on his family. "Mary, what wonderful children we have. I haven't heard a murmur out of either one of them."

"Why Daddy, we're having the times of our lives," said Elise gaily.

"Same here!" Chris tried to say, guiltily choking over his glass of water, and having to retire behind his napkin. He felt in his heart that it was not quite honest for him to say that. But he couldn't bear not to be a good sport when his father and mother were so wonderful. Well, he was going to get that job in the grocery if it were a possible thing.

He helped Elise clear the table and put the dishes in order, and about half past eight he took his hat and went out.

"Oh, I thought we'd all go to bed early," said his mother looking at him in a troubled way as he opened the door.

"I won't be long, Mother," he tried to reassure her, "I want to see a man about a job I heard of. I can't get him any other time. It might turn out to be something."

"Well, come home as soon as you can. You know this is a strange neighborhood and we aren't sure yet what kind of people live around here. I shall worry—"

"No, you won't worry, Mother," said Chris quickly, "You've been a good sport, and you're not going to worry any more."

She looked after him wistfully as he went out, although she summoned a faint smile, but he knew that she was exceedingly weary, and in spite of all her brave smiles and cheery demeanor this day must have been very hard for her. He felt condemned that he had thought so much about his own part of the disappointment.

As he neared the chain store his soul rebelled. How could he go in there and ask for a job recommended by a girl? A poor girl who really knew him very little too? Oughtn't he to go back and get his father to write a letter, or get in touch with the head of all these stores, or do something that would place him on a regular footing, and give him a worth-while salary?

Then suddenly the words of those two obnoxious girls came to him, that he was a snob, and somehow he felt that he would rather stand on his own feet, and work his way into any possible favor, than to try to hang on to the old life with its power and influence. So he held his head up and walked in.

There were still a few last customers keeping the tired salesmen busy, and Natalie in her little glass house was busy, too, counting change and getting her cash register ready for the night. But she smiled at him distantly and briefly, as he stood by the door and waited until she seemed to have a moment of leisure. Then he went over and spoke to her in a low voice, as if he were just another customer.

"Wouldn't you rather I came in Monday morning and went to the manager myself? I don't want to keep you or bother you. And all these men look so doggone tired I hate to butt in on them now."

"No," said Natalie quickly, "he expects you. I found a chance to tell him you were coming. I didn't say much. I thought you'd rather do your own talking. I just said I knew a man who wanted work and I had told him to come around. He seemed relieved. He's been worried all day about it, but he had no time to go out and look up anybody, and the district manager went to New York yesterday, so he can't call on him for an extra man. There he is now over by those crates, opening them. Now is as good a time as any to talk to him. There aren't many customers left. His name is Foster."

Chris summoned his nerve and walked over to the young fellow in the white linen coat and apron. Why, he didn't look much older than himself!

"Is this Mr. Foster?" he asked, trying to remember that he was asking a favor, not granting one, by being willing to work in that store. "I heard you needed a man. Would I do?"

Foster looked up and eyed Chris keenly, then grinned at him.

"Take hold and help me put these cans on the shelves,

and let's see how you can work," he said. "After that we'll talk."

Chris flung his cap on a barrel top and set to work stacking the cans in orderly rows on the shelves, saying nothing, but taking great armfuls from the crates and stalking back and forth as if his life depended on it. Foster did not appear to be watching him, did not even seem to be aware of him except now and then for a necessary direction, and they worked away as if they had always done this. Chris found that it was actually interesting to put those cans in their ranks quickly and get back for another load in record time.

When the crates were empty Foster gave him another grin.

"That's all. You seem to have pep enough. Just take those empty crates down cellar, door over to your right, smash them up with the ax you'll see at the foot of the stairs, and pile them with the other wood against the wall. When you come back we'll talk business."

When Chris came upstairs the customers were gone and the front door closed. Natalie was putting on her hat and coat in her little glass den.

Foster had a pencil and note book and began asking him questions. His name, age, experience, was he a stranger, was he willing to obey orders?

Chris answered briefly, and studied his new boss. A quick keen alert young man without conceit. He liked him.

"All right," said Foster, "you report Monday morning at eight o'clock. You understand I haven't authority to hire you permanently. But I'll try you out for a week and report to my boss when he gets back next week. If you make good I'll be glad to have you. You worked well to-night. Good night. See you Monday," and the interview was over.

Chris went out just behind Natalie and they walked down the street together, she a little shy and beaming.

"He liked you, I could see," she said.

"I guess you've been saying something pretty nice about me," said Chris gratefully. "That was awfully fine of you. I appreciate it. If I get the job I guess I'll owe it to you."

"Oh, I just told him you were all right, steady and dependable you know. He used to know my grandmother and my father, and he knows I wouldn't say that if it were not so." Natalie walked gravely beside him putting aside her part in the matter as if it were very slight. "I told him we had been in the same school and you always had good marks."

"Well, I won't forget it," he said with a friendly smile. "Say, let me carry that bundle. Sorry I haven't any car anymore to take you home."

"Oh, I'm used to bundles," she laughed. "You mustn't go out of your way for me. We're just fellow laborers. You mustn't feel that way about it. A working girl has to carry her own bundles."

"Not if there is a gentleman about," said Chris masterfully possessing himself of the heavy carton she was carrying.

"You'll have your own bundles to carry presently," she said. "You know the employees get a low price on things, and sometimes there are perishable things Saturday nights that they let us have for almost nothing. I save a lot that way carrying things home."

"I suppose you do," said Chris thoughtfully, "I hadn't even thought about saving on things like that. I guess I'll have to take lessons of you. Though my mother used to tell us stories about how they lived on very little when she was a girl."

"She'll know then," assured the girl. "It doesn't take

long to learn to save. But, really, you mustn't go out of your way for me. Please let me take it now. This is my corner."

"It's not out of my way," said Chris gravely, "You didn't know I lived on the next street to yours, did you?"

"Oh!" said Natalie, startled. Then *"Oh!"* in a sorrowful little voice, "I'm sorry you had to leave that lovely home. I always enjoyed looking at it. I saw your mother coming out of the door one day. She's beautiful. I thought she fitted there so well. I liked to think of her living in such lovely surroundings. My mother had a nice home too, when she was young."

Chris looked down on her with interested eyes, his heart warming toward her because she admired his mother, and because she was sorry about his lost home. There seemed somehow a bond between them.

"I guess it's hard for a girl," he hesitated shyly, fumbling around in his mind for the right words, "to grow up,—not having everything she wants."

"Oh, I don't know," said Natalie with her gay little laugh again. "We've had some wonderful good times. When Father was alive we used to enjoy what we did have, much more than some people seem to who have everything. But, it was always nice to hear Mother tell about the hardwood floors and oriental rugs and lovely things they had in her home when she was a girl. Of course, when we didn't have things we usually made them somehow if it was possible."

"It's a rotten deal for a girl like you to have to do that," he said impulsively.

She looked up at him surprised.

"Why, no! I don't think so," she said gravely.

"You don't think so?" It was his turn to be surprised.

"Not at all." Her tone almost held reproof. "Nothing that God allows to come to His children is a rotten deal.

He loves us and knows what we need most. He wouldn't let it come to us if it wasn't for our best."

"You believe He sends such things then?"

"He lets them come," she said seriously. "Nothing can come to us unless it first passes through His hands." There was a sweet trustfulness about her tone that filled him with sudden reverence toward her. "Of course some of the hard things are testings for us, but He permits them, and what He permits must be best for us."

"What possible good could come out of your having to be poor and work for your living, and carry bundles too heavy for you?"

"Well," said Natalie with sudden whimsical laughter, "It might be to keep me from being a snob. I'm afraid I would have been an awful snob if I had had a lovely home and all the nice things some girls have."

"You?" said Chris wonderingly, and then he laughed too. "Do you know, I just heard myself called a snob, this afternoon, back there in the store, by two little snub-nosed, lipsticked flappers that used to be in the Grammar school when we were in High."

"I know who you mean. But they only thought so because you weren't fresh with them the way some of the other boys were. You never were a snob. You were always kind and pleasant to everybody. Look how you picked me up and took me home with all my bundles in your beautiful new car."

"But why shouldn't I?"

"That's it," said Natalie, decidedly, "You're a gentleman. You never were a snob. Now Bob Tyson wouldn't have done that. He wouldn't even have seen me as he whizzed by."

"Well," said Chris, "it's comforting that you didn't think I was a snob. But I'm not so sure I wasn't in a fair way to become one, come to think of it. You see your instance of my courtesy wasn't a fair one, for I recognized the lady in you. I'm not so sure I'd have picked up those two flappers even if they had a whole truck load to carry. So, you think the raw deal that has been handed out to me is to teach me something, do you? You think I ought to be thankful for it? Losing my home and my college diploma and my car and everything that makes life worth while?"

"You haven't lost your home," said Natalie quickly, "nor your father and mother and sister. You still have a place to live, and I'm pretty sure it's a real home even if it isn't as big and elegant as it used to be. And maybe there are bigger and better things than college diplomas in life."

Chris stared.

"Say, you talk like the fellow that preached in our church the last Sunday before the crash. He said we ought to be thankful for everything that's handed out. But I didn't know anybody ever really took it to heart."

"Yes," said Natalie simply, "he's wonderful. He has charge of the Mission down in Water Street. Did you ever go down there? It's very interesting."

"No," said Chris shortly, "but I guess if he had a little of the hardness he's talking about handed out to him he'd sing a different tune. I don't see singing praise when the earth is reeling under you. He doesn't know what he's talking about."

"Yes, he knows," said Natalie sadly, "He lost his wife and two little children of small pox over in China. He was a missionary there. He's only back on a year's furlough on account of a very severe operation he had to have. He's going back in a couple of months now, going to take charge of a leper hospital, and doesn't expect ever to return to this country. But he's a great man, and he knows what it is to praise God under heavy trial. He calls it 'singing in the rain.'"

"Good night!" said Chris earnestly, "I guess I'd better shut up. I'm not even in the same class with a man like that. He must be some kind of super man."

"No," said Natalie quickly, "he's only an ordinary man with a great God. God can do great things with people who are willing to let Him."

They had reached Natalie's door now, and Chris handed her the bundles.

"Well, you sure have given me something to think about," he said gravely. "Good night, and thank you more than I can tell for what you have done for me."

NATALIE'S mother looked at her anxiously as she came in, noticed the bright color in her cheeks, the light in her eyes, and sighed.

"Did someone come home with you, dear?" she asked guardedly.

Natalie turned a disarming smile on her mother and put down her armful of bundles.

"Why, yes, Mother," she said happily. "I don't know how I should have managed all these bundles if he hadn't. My arm has been aching like the dickens all day where I twisted it wrestling with that window with the broken cord last night. Just look what I've got, Mother, a whole lot of celery! Isn't that great? It has just been frosted on the outside and turned brown and doesn't sell very well in consequence, but the heart of it is as sweet as can be. I tasted some and it's wonderful. We can make apple salad, and meat salad, and celery soup and a lot of things besides eating the best of it just plain."

"It wasn't one of the store men, was it, Natalie?" asked her mother as she wiped her hands on the roller towel and came over to look at the celery. "I wouldn't encourage them to get intimate if I were you. It isn't wise. If you let one of them come home with you another might, and you don't know what they are all like. Even if we have to go without some things I wouldn't bring so much you can't carry it yourself. Or—of course, sometimes Janice might come up and meet you about closing time."

"Oh, Motherie dear!" laughed Natalie stooping to kiss her little mother. "Don't you worry. Every one of those boys in the store is nice and pleasant and courteous. They don't hire any other kind there. And they all have their girls. You don't need to worry about me. They don't want to go with me. They tell me about their girls every chance they get, at noon time or in the morning. They say where they went the night before, and ask my advice about what to get them for Christmas. I'm a regular old maid auntie in the store, so I'm perfectly safe. Nobody thinks of me there as a girl you know, I'm just the cashier. But this wasn't one of them. At least he isn't yet, though he's going to be Monday morning. They've just hired him. Mother, it was Chris Walton!"

"Chris Walton! Again!" said the mother with a strange alarm in her voice. "Oh, Natalie, I'm just afraid you will get interested in him! Why does he keep coming around you?"

Janice appeared in the front room doorway then:

"What do you mean, Natty, Chris Walton working in the store? Your store? How did he come to do that? Goodness! You'd think his father could get him a different job in some bank or lawyer's office or something, wouldn't you? Mother, did you hear what Natalie said? Chris Walton is going to work in the chain store."

"Oh," said the mother in perplexity, "Not *really?* Is that what you said, Natalie? How strange!"

"Isn't it?" said Natalie. "I couldn't believe he would.

He's always seemed so exclusive, and somehow remote. But he came into the store this afternoon to buy bread, and—"

"Natalie, has he been coming there to meet you?" asked her mother, quick to apprehend any possible danger to her offspring.

"Why, no, of course not," said Natalie shortly, her brow quite vexed looking. "How silly! Why he didn't even know I was there till he came up to pay his check, and then he stopped a minute and said he was looking for a job. He hasn't gone back to college, Mother, though it's his senior year. He said he had walked all over the city and couldn't find anything to do *anywhere,* and he laughingly asked me if I knew of a job. Of course then I had to tell him we had an opening right there in the store, just came that day. It was Tom Bonar's job. He's the one with the red hair you know. He got a telegram that his father had died and he had to go back to Wisconsin right away and stay with his mother, and our manager has been terribly upset about it all day because he didn't know where to turn for the right man. I didn't suppose Chris would look at it or think about it, but he seemed so terribly in earnest that I had to let him know about it. But Mother, he just jumped at the chance. He was real humble about it. Said he was right down at the foot of the ladder ready to do anything. He had a good spirit, Mother. And so he came back at closing time and they hired him."

"Oh, dear, Natalie, child. I'm afraid you are going to get interested in him. He'll be right there in the store all day, and you'll see him a lot."

"Why shouldn't she get interested in him, Mother?" broke in Janice. "He's a *prince.* I should think you'd be glad she could have such a friend."

"But he'll not stay there," said the anxious mother.

"He'll get some other big thing pretty soon and sail off into his own social standing again, and Natalie will be left lonely and heartbroken!"

"Oh, Mother dear!" said Natalie, "Please, please don't think of me always in terms of matrimony. I have no desire to fall in love or get married or break my heart or any of those tempestuous things. Forget it, and trust God. Chris is just a nice boy I knew a little in school, and there's nothing wrong about his carrying my bundles home once in a while, although I'll manage it of course not to have it necessary. I guess you've brought me up decently, Mother, and I hope you can trust me. Besides, I don't wear my heart on the outside where every passing thing can knock against it and break it. He was only grateful to me for telling him about the job to-night. He probably won't have time to even look at me again. We're busy people in that store, Mother. We haven't time for nonsense. But, here's something. I had a chance to witness for Christ to him to-night," and she told of her conversation with Chris.

When she had finished her mother came and kissed her gently on the forehead.

"Forgive me, dear, for being over anxious. You and Jan are all I have, and I keep fluttering about you like an old hen over her chickens I suppose. I guess I can trust my girl to be careful and discreet, and I am glad you were brave enough to talk with him that way. I've always heard his father and mother were good Christians. His father is an elder in our church you know, but of course I've never known them personally. And you can't tell these days what a son is just by what his father was."

"Well," said Natalie, "I told him about our mission and the Bible School. Maybe he'll go sometime. He seemed interested. Now I suppose you'll go and worry about that. But if Jan fixes her lessons so she can go

Monday nights with me, we'd be together and it isn't in the least likely he'd walk home with us anyway. Mother he's just an old school mate being polite. For pity's sake don't make me so self conscious about him or I'll have to get another job."

"No, no, I won't dear," said the mother quickly, "I shouldn't have spoken at all I suppose, only I'm so afraid for you, and so sorry about you that you can't have the right companionship."

"I should worry about companions!" said Natalie gaily. "I've got Jan, haven't I? What's better than a perfectly good sister? Is that cocoa on the stove? Look, it's boiling over! My, I'm hungry. These late Saturday hours and the rush at dinner time make me like a little starved street child. Oh, and you've got toast and eggs for me! Isn't that great? Can't you all sit down and eat something too?"

"Yes," said Janice, "We saved our oranges from this morning, and yours too. You didn't eat yours at breakfast, you know, so we are going to eat together."

Then the three sat down to a simple little meal in the neat white kitchen, and had as good a time as if they had been three girls, chatting and planning.

But just before they went upstairs to bed Mrs. Halsey said:

"Natalie, I'm sorry I said what I did. I don't want you to think I don't trust you, and I am glad of the way you are using your influence with that young man. We'll all pray for him, shall we, that he may find the Lord and get to know Him?"

"Oh, yes, Mother. That will be wonderful. We'll claim that promise, 'Where two of you shall agree' won't we? Mother, he would be a power if he were really saved. You know of course he's a member of the church like most of the rest of the young folks that go to our church, but the way he talked I don't think he ever prays or reads his Bible, and it seemed as if he didn't really believe anything much. He spoke as if it were just all a big lot of guesswork, and it might as well be any other religion as Christianity. It isn't likely I'll have another chance to speak about it to him. He'll probably go his own way after to-night. But we can pray and that will reach him without his knowing we have anything to do with it."

"Dear child!" said the mother with a loving look at her eldest daughter.

Meantime Chris had walked thoughtfully, briskly, down the street. As he neared his own door he remembered that he had a job, and he began to whistle cheerfully. His mother heard him as she was hanging up the cleansed dish towels on a little string line above the range, and smiled. It was the first time she had heard her boy whistle since the crash came.

"Well," announced Chris as he came in, "I guess I've landed a job at last. Is isn't Manager of the Standard Oil Company, nor president of the Rockefeller Foundation, but I guess it'll provide at least salt enough for our meals."

His father looked up from the evening paper, a light of pleasure in his eyes. His mother came in and beamed at him, and Elise appeared in the doorway behind her eagerly.

"What is it?" asked his sister.

He took a deep breath as if he were about to plunge into a cold ocean, and said:

"Errand boy in the chain store!" and then watched them keenly to get their first reaction.

"A grocery?" said his sister aghast.

"Fine!" said his father quickly.

"'That's a clean nice business," said his mother interestedly.

Then Elise with bright, fond eyes, smiling at him:

"I'm proud of you, Chrissy!"

Chris drew another deep breath, this time of relief, and grinned.

"Well, don't get too set up," he said sheepishly, "they're only going to try me out Monday. They may not keep me. I may prove too good for 'em, see?"

They had family worship, Father giving thanks for Chris's prospects, and then they all went to bed upstairs in the funny little crowded rooms, where even a bed and a small old-fashioned bureau made too many things in the room. Boy! but he had a game family! Look how they took his grocery job! Even Elise, who, being in school might be kidded about it! They amused themselves calling back and forth to one another through the thin partitions, and trying to make a joke of the strangeness, but after all there was a hominess about it that had a pleasant side. Even Chris had a throb of thanksgiving as he realized how sane and well and altogether normal his father was. In fact now he thought about it his father was more cheerful than he had been for the past year or so. Probably the bank's affairs had been growing more and more complicated, and worried him, and now it was good to be down to rock bottom and try to climb up bravely again.

On the whole Chris felt happier than he had since the trouble came. He got into bed with a pleasant thump of his pillow, and a gay good night to them all. But he did not sleep at once. He began to think of Natalie and what she had said. What an unusual girl she was. Not at all the shy mouse of a thing she had seemed in school. He wished he had known her before when he was in a position to show her some nice times. It would have been fun to give her rides and take her to class entertainments and parties. Now he thought of it he couldn't remember ever having seen her at one. Probably the girls had high-hatted her too. Well, she had a lot more to her than any of them. If he ever got the chance he'd let them all know it, too.

Queer things she had said about God, and being thankful for the hard things in her life. He didn't know another girl who would talk like that. He wondered how she got that way, and fell asleep thinking how well she had answered everything he had said. Well, perhaps there was something in it after all. Dad seemed to have something to lean upon. He couldn't understand what it was. He vaguely wished he knew.

Then he gave a bitter thought or two to his old High School friends off in college. Not a line to him about their frats, or how the last football game had gone. Never a cheering word, or regret that he was not with them. Oh, at first of course, that time they came after him, but when they found they couldn't carry him off in triumph to be their hero in college as he had been, that was the end.

True, he hadn't written to them, but that was different. He hadn't anything to write about.

Suddenly he knew as plainly as if a voice had spoken it that their ways had parted definitely. Life had swept them into separate worlds. Would it ever bring them into touch again?

9

WHEN Natalie started for the store on Monday morning she noticed a man standing at the corner of the street with his hat drawn down over his eyes and a watch in his hand.

A look of annoyance passed over her face. That same man had been there three times before watching her come out of the house, almost as if he were waiting for her, timing her. He always gave her an ugly, familiar look as she passed, though she never seemed to notice him. She shrank from encountering it again. He was a big, tough looking man, and she felt almost afraid of him, although it seemed absurd in broad daylight on a street where many people passed.

Impulsively she turned the other way and walked around a whole block to escape him, but when she reached the avenue there he was again at the next corner, standing in just the same position watching her, but this time with an ugly, amused leer on his face as if he wanted to let her know that he knew she had gone out of her way to escape him.

She turned her face the other way and tried to act as

if she had not seen him. It was getting on her nerves to have him do this way. The expression of his face somehow made her shudder. Perhaps he had no idea of watching her at all. Perhaps it was all her imagination.

And then as if to answer her thought, the man spoke. "Hello, Girlie! Can't get away from me, can ya?" he said, and her heart beat wildly. For an instant she wanted to run, but her feet felt like lead, and it occurred to her that she must control herself and walk steadily. She must not let him know she was frightened. She had made a mistake of course going out of her way. He must have seen her hesitate at her own door and then turn the other way to avoid him. She would not do that again. She would just hold up her head and walk by him as if he were not there. Perhaps she ought to warn Janice. It would be terrible if he got to bothering Jan on her way to school.

She forced herself to walk on steadily down the avenue, but she was trembling so she could scarcely stand up.

She made a distinct effort to put the man out of her thoughts. She would not look back to see if he were following her. He was probably just a common fellow without very high standards. There was nothing to be really afraid of, and of course there were policemen whom she could call upon if he attempted to follow her. She might report it to the one that often came into the store. It was just as well to have a man like that cleared out of a neighborhood. It really wasn't safe for a fifteen year old girl like Janice to have to pass such a man. Of course Janice would have to learn to take care of herself too, but somehow she felt ages older than her sister, and as if she must protect her. Above all she must not let her mother find out that that man had spoken to her. It would frighten her so that she would be anxious all the time either of them were away from the house.

She tried to concentrate her thoughts on the dress she was planning for Janice; on the other dress she meant to make possible for Janice's commencement next spring. She wondered how much she dared put away each week from her meager salary to save for that time? She herself hadn't minded so much staying out of the activities of her school at commencement time, but she hated to have Jan miss everything. Jan did love good times so much, and she had so few of them. Jan had been so sweet and good about staying out of school while Mother was sick, and now that Mother was well enough to be left alone all day, she did hope that Jan could have a little more freedom. Work would come soon enough. Also now that Mother didn't have to have extra food and medicine and a doctor all the time there would be more chance of saving a little for a spring wardrobe for Janice. It was so hard for Janice to always wear madeovers because she was the smallest one in the family. For once she should have a dress, perhaps two, which she might go to the store and pick out for herself and try on.

Suddenly the thought of the man burst into her thoughts again. What if he should hang around and frighten Mother? It was silly of course to think that, and what could she do about it but pray? "Oh, God, take care of Mother dear, and Janice, please," she prayed again and again, as she walked down the street, her heart gradually growing quieter and more trustful, her nerves steadying.

As she neared the store she remembered Chris. Would he really come there to work that day, or would he back out of it after thinking it over? Somehow she couldn't make it seem real that Chris Walton, the banker's son, the most popular boy in High School, popular too she had heard in his college, should be coming to work that morning in the store just as she was: to measure sugar and potatoes, and bring up kegs of mackerel from the cellar. Probably when his people found it out they would put a stop to it. Probably his lady mother would do something about it. She would want him in a profession. But anyway, Natalie told herself, she was glad that Chris himself had been willing to do any good honest work. It fitted so perfectly with the ideal she had formed of his character as she had watched him from afar through four years of High School. Natalie like to keep her ideals of people she admired. Her standards were high and not many came up to them. So far this young man had. She would likely never have much to do with him. Her life and his were as far apart as the poles of course. Even if he came into the store for a time there would presently be found something else for him, something more in the line of a profession, and this little spurt of work in a store would only be used as a stepping stone to something fitter. But if he came, while he stayed, she hoped he would make good. He would never be anything to her of course, but she liked to think there were such fine noble people in the world, a few such young men. It made the world more worth while to live in.

Of course he had been kind to her, and just now he happened to be grateful to her for having put him on to the position, but she mustn't presume upon that. She must keep her quiet aloof way. Her act of introducing him to the manager had been the merest trifling kindness. Anyone would do that. She mustn't let him think that she was expecting him to pay her any attention whatever. Indeed, she must manage to get away before he did, so that it would not look that way. He must not think he had to carry her bundles home for her.

However, if he came, and if he stayed, he would probably soon be so busy he wouldn't think anything about it. The routine of the day would take care of that. He would be so tired by evening that he would want to get home quickly, and wouldn't have time for the little cashier. She needn't worry about that. She only hoped he would make good,—if he came.

But he was there before her, waiting outside the store, and they stood together talking for a minute or two. It was very pleasant to have him so friendly, the boy whom all the girls had admired. And she couldn't blame them. She had admired him herself always. Had liked to listen to him recite in school because he always did it as if he enjoyed it and knew what he was talking about. She had seldom had the pleasure of going to a school game because she had always had to hurry home to help her mother right after school, but she had often stood at the schoolroom window at recess with a book spread on the window sill before her, and watched the boys practicing in the yard below. And always she had singled out Chris as the most finished player, and exulted in the way he led them all, and they deferred to him. Well, now she was enjoying a pleasant little contact with one whom she could have enjoyed as a friend if their circumstances in life had been different, but she must not let her head get turned by it. He was Chris Walton and she was Natalie Halsey, born into different worlds and stations. Of course her family had been good too, but the world had forgotten that, though all the families of the earth were one after all! But then, she knew what people thought of a poor girl allowing a friendship with a boy who was in a higher social class, and she didn't intend to put herself in such a position. So, as soon as the store was opened she retired to her little glass den and began to work with her cash register and her books, and Chris stood back by a counter, and watched the day in the store open before him.

It interested him that he was to be a part of this busy new world.

Almost at once people began to swarm in, for coffee and butter and yeast cakes, for a loaf of bread, and a box of Aunt Jemima's prepared buckwheat, for cereals, dried beef and glasses of jelly for lunches.

There came a little lull in half an hour and the manager started him to work, gave him a linen coat and an apron, set him to picking over a barrel of potatoes, and putting them up in paper sacks, so many pounds to a sack. There was to be a bargain sale of potatoes that day. And when the potatoes were all measured he had a barrel of lettuce to go over and pick out the perfect heads. Queer bitter thoughts came to him now and then as he remembered the other boys in his class all in college now, going about with college caps, whistling on the campus as they went from one class to another, wearing their fraternity pins and planning their pleasant careers for the future, while he sorted decaying vegetables.

But for the most part Chris was rather interested than otherwise in what he had to do, conscientious to do it thoroughly, and ambitious to see how quickly he could get it done. He was too busy to contemplate the fate that had thrown him into a chain grocery instead of a college.

Now and then he cast a glance over at the little glass den where Natalie worked, busy every minute, making change, smiling pleasantly at the customers, a crowd always around her little window. How patient and sweet she looked. Her delicate face shone out, too fine for such surroundings. Of course the store was nice and clean, and the people were all decent respectable people, and there was nothing really unpleasant about her work, but somehow she looked a lady, made to be waited upon. There was a quiet refinement about her. What was that nursery rhyme Elise used to sing, "Sit on a cushion and sew a fine seam, and feed upon strawberries, sugar and cream." Somehow Natalie's face made one feel like putting her at ease, and caring for her.

So Chris's thoughts moved in and out all day between the cabbages he brought up from the cellar and the empty crates and cans that he carried down cellar. He was literally an errand boy as he had said, taking orders moment by moment, never through with one activity before another was handed him. By noon he was hungry as a bear and ready to devour eagerly the hot coffee and sandwiches that the manager had sent in for his helpers from the pie shop near by because he couldn't spare any of them at that hour to go out and get it for themselves.

They bolted the food standing in the back room where the stores were kept, leaning back against the big refrigerator, or sitting on the cellar stairs or an empty crate, swallowed it down hastily, one at a time in turn, and hastened back to work again. Chris wondered that they had so much business all the time. He had never supposed that a grocery store would be such an active place. There seemed always to be somebody wanting something. By night he was dog-weary and sore in every muscle. Some muscles he hadn't known he possessed. And he had thought that every muscle he had was in perfect training. He wondered why it seemed so much more strenuous than playing football. Perhaps because it was utterly new, and he was a little excited about it, anxious to please.

He heard that first day that the district manager would be around in the middle of the week and his fate would probably be decided then. The district manager would possibly have a new man to put in the place, and Chris being only a substitute would have to step out.

That made it a sort of game, and Chris worked harder than ever. He might not have picked out the grocery business for a life work, and he might not want to remain in it forever, but he didn't want to be put out of anything he had undertaken. He wanted to be so good that they would beg him to stay, even if he was leaving of his own free will for a better position. So he pitched into his work with all his might.

He discovered that his fellow workmen were most friendly among themselves, but that they regarded him with suspicion. He had not yet won their confidence. He had that to do. They regarded him as an entire outsider. Perhaps some inkling of his former estate had already penetrated to their knowledge.

They answered him shortly, gave him no more information regarding his work than was absolutely necessary, left him to find out for himself in every case possible. They let him search for an article in the cellar instead of telling him how close it was to his hand, and were generally just as unpleasant as they could be without actually descending to open fight.

Chris was rather amazed at first, and then indignant. He longed to take them out and thrash them one by one. He found his heart in a continual fume over some rudeness or unnecessary taunt.

It did not help his course that on the third day of his presence in the store there came an influx of young women, three of them. They were dressed up apparently for an afternoon tea. They breezed in holding their dainty chiffons and handsome fur coats back from the barrels and boxes. Somewhat affectedly they demanded to see Christopher Walton.

CHRIS was cleaning the cellar. He had been at it all day. There was to be a new arrangement of boxes and stores that were kept down there and everything in the whole cellar had to be moved and thoroughly cleaned. He had never done anything quite like it before except the washing of those windows in the Sullivan Street house, but he was working away like mad trying to get done before night. He was wearing a pair of borrowed overalls which did not fit him, and his hair was sticking every way. He was just awkwardly wringing out a wet mop when the man from the meat counter yelled down the cellar stairs:

"Hey, there, Walton! Some dames up here wantta see ya! Make it snappy!"

Chris dropped his mop in dismay and stared up the stairs.

"I can't come!" he shouted at the disappearing heels of his informant, but the only answer that came back was another:

"Make it snappy! The boss hates a mess of ladies around in the way. This ain't no social tea!"

Angrily Chris started up the stairs, wiping his wet hands on his overalls each side, and dashing them wildly through his disordered hair. What he meant to do was to get a glimpse from the back of the store and see whether this was some practical joke or not. If the boss had sent for him he would go of course, but otherwise he would retreat again to the cellar and pretend not to have heard. Surely neither his mother nor Elise would come to bother him.

But Irene Claskey, Ethel Harrower and Anna Peters had not stayed on the order of their going. They had followed down the length of the store and stood just outside the doorway of the store room into which the cellar stairs led. So he came upon them before he realized, and they all clamored at once:

"Hello, Chris! Congratulations!" they screeched.

"So it's really true! You've got a job! How long will it last?"

"Oh, Chris but you're a scream. Whose overalls are those? Did you borrow them from your butler?"

And then they let out a wild hilarious laughter that arrested the attention of everyone in the crowded store.

White with fury Chris stood glaring at them, his chin lifted haughtily. Every eye was upon him now. Even the boss coming down that way with a grin on his pleasant face. The boss had been fine. He must do something about this.

"Did you want something?" he asked in a clear stern voice. Even Natalie heard him away up at the front of the store in her little glass den. His voice was so impersonal that you might have thought he was merely addressing a customer.

"Sure thing we want something!" clanged out Irene, rather enjoying her large audience than otherwise, and openly exulting in Chris's discomfiture. "We're going to have a High School reunion next Saturday night, and we want you to help us out. We're having a spree up at the Rabbitt Inn on Horndale Pike, and we want you to take a bunch up there."

"I haven't got any car!" said Chris shortly.

"Oh, we know that," went on Irene. "We can get a car if you'll drive it. Dad said you were a good driver and he'd trust our car with you. We have to start at five o'clock and we're meeting at my house—"

But Chris stopped her voluble details with a clear ringing word.

"Nothing doing!" he said firmly. "Sorry to seem unaccommodating but I have to work. Good afternoon!" and he turned on his heel and vanished down the cellar stairs, shutting the door behind him.

The customers turned back to their bargains with smiles and knowing looks toward the discomfited girls who stared for a moment, and then with many giggles and contemptuous remarks picked their way hilariously out of the store.

Chris stayed down cellar the rest of the afternoon and worked like a fiend. He had no mind to go upstairs and be kidded by the entire store force. He made that cellar look like a parlor. The floor was scrubbed clean enough to eat from. Every box and crate was set with mathematical exactness, arranged in logical order, each row was labeled with a number on the beam overhead and the same number chalked on each container. The cellar was so systematized that anything could be found in a jiffy. But Chris had been working with only one half of his well-trained mind. The other half had been raging, rending him, lashing itself in fury over his humiliation. Those girls! Fools! he called them, and took out his revenge on the cellar floor, using up to the handle the bristles of the old scrubbing brush. Never was cellar floor so clean before.

When all the others had gone home the boss came down and looked around well pleased and full of commendation. Chris listened in silence to his comments of praise for the way he had arranged things, and then he burst forth.

"I'm all kinds of sorry, Mr. Foster, that those fool girls came around and made a scene. They're not any special friends of mine and they just wanted to play some kind of a joke on me I guess. I certainly was sore."

"Oh, that's all right, Chris," said the boss, a warm light coming into his eyes. "I understand. Some girls are just naturally made that way. Don't you worry. You've done good work this afternoon. Forget the other. You did 'em up all righty, and I was glad to see it. They hustled away after you left them, like a row of little dogs with their tails tucked in. They certainly didn't get a rise out of you."

Chris looked up with his heart warming toward this young man who was his superior, and grinned. It was the first time he had called him Chris, and somehow he did not resent it. It seemed rather pleasant.

"Thank you," he said heartily, "It's great of you to take it that way. One thing's certain. I don't want anything more to do with those girls, never did have much, only we were in the same class in school."

"Well, they're no ladies," said Foster, "Now take our Miss Halsey, she's a lady. She may not wear such high-falutin' clothes, nor train around to parties, and she may have to work for her living, but when it comes to acting like a lady, boy, she can put it all over those other three. She's a fine girl."

"She certainly is," said Chris heartily, and felt a queer little thrill of pleasure at hearing Natalie commended.

"Well," said Foster, "guess it's time for us to quit to-night. You've made this cellar look like a palace and no mistake. You're going to make a go of it here, I can see that already. Well, good night!"

Chris went home that night walking on air. His boss had commended him, and had actually hinted that his job was practically a sure thing. He was surprised at himself that he cared so much to keep it.

He had almost forgotten about the unpleasant incident of the girls that afternoon, till suddenly it occurred to him that he had not seen Natalie all day except at a distance. She hadn't waited for him. Perhaps she had heavy bundles to carry and had to carry them herself with her slender little arms. In the only glimpse he had caught of her she looked white and tired. He wondered if her mother had perhaps been worse, and she had been up all night with her. He found a distinct cause for worry in the thought.

Then he began to wonder if Natalie had seen those girls. Of course she must have. She could not have missed them. No one could. That fiendish Irene had taken care of that. Did Natalie think that was the kind of girls he liked? Did she perhaps hear their invitation and think he was going to accept it and take those girls to a class spree at that infamous road house, Rabbitt Inn on Horndale Pike! Somehow he did not want Natalie to think he was intimate with those girls.

Of course he had known Irene Claskey and Anna Peters since kindergarten days, but Ethel Harrower was a comparatively new arrival in town with a rather unclassed social standing. None of the girls but Irene and Ethel had taken her up. She used too much rouge and lipstick and smoked a good deal in public. People like Mrs. Walton didn't consider her nice. Somehow it gave him an unpleasant feeling to think that Natalie had

supposed her his friend. Was that the reason Natalie had
hurried home? He wished he knew. He would try and
get out early the next morning and get a chance to speak
to her in the store before people began to come. Though
it had been his policy, and hers too, apparently, to keep
their distance. Well, perhaps he could catch up to her on
the way and get a word with her. He wasn't just clear
what he could say. He was too well bred to just sail in
and blast those other girls. Yet he certainly did not want
Natalie to think he belonged to that crowd. Well, it
wouldn't be long till to-morrow now, and anyhow he
was glad at what the boss had said. He would tell Natalie
that. She would be pleased too.

So he whistled cheerily as he went up the walk to the
little old clapboard house that looked so desolate on the
outside, and was so cheery and shabby inside.

His father looked up at the sound and said to his
mother:

"Our boy is coming through in good shape after all,
Mary." And she smiled, motherwise, and said:

"I knew he would, didn't you?"

They had a cheery supper that night in spite of simple
fare. The mother was resurrecting all her old recipes,
plain wholesome food, cheaply bought and deriving its
savory taste and smell from the old deftness in seasoning,
the trick of long cooking, and careful preparation. Perhaps because of its very difference from what they had
been eating for years, its simplicity rather charmed the
family. Bean soup made with tomatoes, potatoes and
celery tops, a "mess of pottage" the mother called it;
brown bread; baked apples and cream; even bread pudding with a dash of chocolate to make it tasty; hash! Yes,
they loved it, Mother's hash. That was different. Mother
could make hash taste like stuffed turkey. It all seemed
so good and they were so hungry from their work, for

Elise had found a job of looking after two small children afternoons after school, and she came in from riding them up and down the streets in their express wagon tired and hungry and happy over the fifty cents she had earned. Elise was standing up well under the family calamity.

When they had finished the bean-tomato soup and the baked apples were served, Chris told them in an off-hand sort of way about what the manager had said to him.

Chris couldn't quite comprehend the look of utter joy in his father's face. He didn't see why he should be so moved when he tried to speak.

"Chris, son, that is great. You've won a bigger battle this week than ever you won in school or on the football field. You've got into the game of life now, and you've begun to conquer yourself. You've made good in a game you didn't like and didn't want to play and under circumstances that were most trying. Don't think I haven't understood."

"But Dad," interrupted Chris, "I—you—"

"It's no use trying to deceive me, boy," said the father laying his hand tenderly on his son's arm, "Your mother and I knew how hard it was for you to give up college and go to work. That kind of hard uninteresting work, too, and to which you were so unaccustomed. We dreaded it for you more than you possibly could for yourself. We had great ambitions for you, Chris. You know that. You are our only son, and there was no height too high for us to dream of your scaling. But I've come to see, through my own humiliations, that one cannot grow strong without being humble. One cannot do great things while self interest rules. You, my son, have gained one great victory this week over self. I hope it may go on. There are still greater heights to scale. You will have setbacks. You'll find that self is a hard thing to conquer. It will come alive. But if you have really found that you can set self aside and do the thing well that is hardest for you, you have reached a great place in life. There is but one thing higher than that, and that is to let the Lord Christ come in and take Self's place. If you can learn those two things I shall know why God let all this reversal come to us. I have known all along that there must be some reason why we should thank Him for what has come, and now I begin to see a possible reason."

Chris looked at his father in amazement, a deep embarrassment upon him, a sudden feeling that he had always been a failure as a son in his father's eyes.

"Why Dad," he said huskily, deeply moved, "I didn't know—I never thought—that you felt that way."

"Well, I do, son, and your mother feels that way too. Go on and win the game of life. Let Christ come into your life as the ruling power, and we shall be too proud to contain ourselves."

Chris thought about it when he went up to bed, thought how his father had spoken in much the same way that Natalie had talked. In fact, there were three of them, for there was that minister who had said we must thank God for hard things. The minister, and Father, and Natalie! All saying the same thing. Was it possible that God had been sending these things into his life for a special purpose? Possible that God, a great God—if there really was one—had thought enough of his little individual life among all the lives of the earth, to turn the affairs of a great bank upside down, and bring changes into other people's lives, with any thought of its affecting him in his relation to himself, to life, and to God Himself? And yet, most of the professors and students at college felt that if there was a God at all He was only a sort of impersonal force. Well, it was worth thinking about. Somehow the idea did not make him angry either, as it had done a week ago.

He went to sleep thinking what Natalie had told him of that missionary's life and bitter disappointments, thinking of Natalie's face when she had said: "What He permits must be best for us." And what was that other phrase she used in speaking about the missionary: "He's only an ordinary man with a great God."

The last thing he remembered as he dropped away into slumber was the earnestness in Natalie's eyes as she had said it, and the way her soft hair fell about her forehead. And he decided that the first thing in the morning he would tell her what the boss had said to him last night. She had got the job for him, she had a right to know that he was making good with the manager.

He hurried through his breakfast, and away that he might catch her and walk with her to the store, but when he passed her corner he saw only an ugly looking young bum standing there with his hat down over his eyes, peering out and up the street. A quick look ahead told Chris that Natalie had already got the start of him and was far on her way.

The boss was just unlocking the door as he reached the store, and although it was early Natalie slipped into her glass den at once, with only a little distant smile for Chris, and went to work as if she were very busy.

Chris felt a distinct drooping of his spirits. Now why did Natalie have to act like that? Was it just because those other girls had come in and asked for him? Was she perhaps ashamed of him because he had had such visitors? She didn't want to be known as having anything to do with him? Well, if she felt that way he wouldn't bother her. He held his head high and went to the boss for his orders, unhappiness in his heart and eyes.

They put him to measuring out sugar in small quantities in paper bags. All day long he measured out sugar and rice and put them up in small packages. He worked with set lips and said nothing to anybody. The other men in the store tried to kid him about the "dames" as they called them who had come to visit him, but he maintained an unsmiling silence. If they wanted to be ugly to him, let them. He could keep to himself.

He tried to stay his unhappy mind on the words his father had said to him the night before, and on his mother's satisfied smile, but he had mixed them up so hopelessly in his thoughts with Natalie and her words to him that he got little help from them. He was hurt deeply by Natalie's attitude. All day long he kept utterly out of her sight, thereby deepening her feeling that she ought to keep out of his.

For indeed the visit of those other girls had affected Natalie more than she realized. It made her feel that she had been entirely right in her decision to have nothing to do with Chris, at least of her own accord. These other girls were of course in the same social rank where he belonged. While she never had admired their loud arrogant ways, she knew that most of the town counted them as standing high in the social scale, and would regard her as an outsider. Chris Walton should never have it to say of her that she chased him after getting him a job in the same store where she worked. As far as she was concerned she would go her own way quietly just as she had gone in school. He probably would soon forget that she existed just as he had apparently done while they were in school together.

The free and easy way in which those bedecked girls yesterday had marched into the store as if they owned the earth and demanded to see him, talking to him in that loud familiar way, had made her see how utterly out of his world she was. He probably liked these girls. They had been among his crowd in school, and knew him so much better than she did. She had just idealized somebody again, as she was always doing, and getting a hard knock when she came to earth and found them human. If she could only keep herself from liking people so much and making them out to be so much better than they were, it would save her many a hard time.

So Natalie kept to her glass den, meekly ate her little sandwich at noon without going out to walk, and sat late at her work in the evening until she was sure Chris was gone. No, nobody either in the store or out should ever be able to say that she had chased an aristocrat!

Chris had slipped away out the back door, after hovering in the shadows of the back room, his hat in his hand, watching to see if Natalie would go. She did not even look up. She wanted to avoid him. Very well, then he would not trouble her. So he went out into the dark street with bitterness in his heart again. All the joy of the night before had left him, and he was downright cross and tired and hungry and disappointed. He didn't care whether he had pleased the boss or not. Self was in the ascendency and he felt that he was being ill treated by Fate or God or somebody. Perhaps it was Natalie.

As he passed the end of Natalie's street there he saw that same tough-looking man standing at the corner watching down the street. Was it possible that he was a friend of Natalie's? Perhaps Natalie was going out with him? Yet he knew in his heart it was not so. And when he had passed on to Sullivan Street, he turned back and saw him still there looking down the street, and even as he watched, the man started down the street toward the store.

Then a sudden frenzy possessed Chris. That man meant no good. He knew a hard-boiled tough when he saw one. Chris hesitated only a second, and then bounded swiftly across the avenue, darted on down Sullivan Street a block and rounded the corner of the street that ended back of the chain store. With the swiftness of a trained athlete he sped till he came to the back of the store, and slid through the alley just beyond.

CHRIS reconnoitered a moment, peering around the corner of the building. He was satisfied that he had reached there a full block ahead of the other man who had loitered as he walked, apparently on purpose. Yes, far up at the next corner he could see a figure lounging under a street light, looking just now back toward Sullivan Street. He was not too late. He peered into the store. Natalie was coming out fastening her coat. The boss was back in the store arranging cans on the counter for to-morrow. Two other men had been detained to help him. He drew a deep breath. Now, should he walk boldly up and speak to her, or should he let her go and follow at a distance to protect her if she needed protection, or at least to watch and discover whether she met this fellow as if he were an acquaintance? She had a right of course to choose her own friends.

Yet as he considered this his feet seemed to carry him of their own volition up to the door of the store as Natalie came out, her arms full of bundles.

As naturally as if he had always done it he stepped up to her and took her bundles.

"Well, you've come at last!" he said, trying to laugh naturally as if she had not kept away from him all day. "I thought maybe you had brought your dinner and over-night bag and meant to stay till to-morrow and save walking home."

"Oh," she said in relieved delight, "Oh, but I thought you had gone home long ago. I was waiting—That is I thought—"

"All right. Say it! Say you were waiting till I got away so you wouldn't have to walk home with me. It's best to be entirely frank even among friends. I wouldn't want to intrude. If you want to know the truth I did start home. Got away up to the corner of Sullivan Street. I'm not entirely blind. It was plain as the nose on your face that you didn't want anything more to do with me after what happened yesterday afternoon. And I didn't intend to bother you anymore of course if you felt that way. But when I got up to the corner of your street I saw a bum standing on the corner right where you had to pass, as if he were waiting, and I couldn't see having you go there alone, so I sprinted around down the alley and came after you. But if I've made a mistake and he's a friend of yours, why just say the word and I'll let you go on your way."

"Oh," said Natalie with a little frightened cry, catching hold of his sleeve impulsively. "Why, I don't feel that way. I'm so glad you came! He tried to speak to me last night and I was so frightened I could hardly get into the house. And I didn't dare tell Mother. She wouldn't have let me come to the store to-day. He's been there for three mornings now, and he called me 'girlie.'"

She caught her breath and he could see that there were tears in her eyes. His heart came right up in his throat and he felt a great righteous anger stirring him, but his voice grew calm and manly sounding.

"Well, if that's the case let's cut through the alley and

go up around the far block and avoid him. I'm here to look out for you. If that dirty sucker shows his face around you, I sure will let him know where to get off. You needn't worry now."

He slid a protecting arm within her own, putting her on his right side away from the watching lounger up the street, and guiding her swiftly through the dark alley and up another block where they could not be seen.

"Now," said he, "if that's the case why haven't you spoken to me all day?"

"Why, I did speak to you. I said good morning!" Natalie gurgled between a sob and a happy little giggle.

"Like an icicle you did!" said Chris grimly. "What had I done to you, I'd like to know? Did you suppose I staged that scene in the store yesterday with me dressed in overalls for the part? Did you suppose I made a date with those fool girls to get the lime light on me before the boss and spoil my chance of keeping the job? Didn't you know those girls just did that to get me in wrong? I never did like that Peters girl anyway. She's crazy, and Irene is always playing to the gallery. The whole thing was, Irene wanted to get it back on me for refusing to take her to a road house one night. She wanted to rub it in that I don't have any car now to take anybody anywhere in. Wanted me to be their chauffeur. Did you hear what she said?"

"I certainly did," said Natalie indignantly, "and—I didn't think any of those things about you—I didn't indeed. I just thought that I—that you—"

"You just thought you didn't want to appear to have anything more to do with me after all that publicity," said Chris bitterly, "I understand, and I don't blame you, but you needn't look quite so much like an icicle. I won't bother you if you don't want to be friends."

"Oh," said Natalie, and now he saw she was crying in

earnest, "I didn't think any such thing. I just thought—after I saw those girls all dressed up—and I knew they belonged to the crowd you used to go with,—and I knew they wouldn't recognize me if they saw me, and wouldn't speak to me if they did,—it just kind of made me see that I wasn't in your—well—social class, and I mustn't make you think I was chasing you and wanting you to walk home with me and carry my bundles all the time. I hate girls to do things like that. I wasn't brought up to do so!"

They had come now to a comparatively quiet block of houses, with no one else about, and their steps slowed down.

"Good night! Natalie, I didn't mean to make you feel that way! Don't cry!" Chris suddenly fumbled in his pocket and brought out a comparatively clean handkerchief. "Here." He shifted his bundles and reaching across them wiped her eyes awkwardly, "as if anybody could ever think *you* were like that! Why, Natalie,—you're wonderful! I think you're just *wonderful!*"

There was a strange new tenderness in his voice. He had a sudden longing to kiss her on her trembling lips and on her sweet wet eyes. But he wasn't a boy who went around kissing girls. His mother had brought him up with fine old-fashioned ideas of reverence for girls, and he felt a deep reverence now for this girl. So he drew her arm closer within his own, caught her hand in a good strong grip, and struggled for new words to make plain what he was feeling.

And Natalie struggled to get her composure.

"Thank you," she said softly, "I thank you. It's nice to feel you are friendly, and haven't misunderstood me or thought me forward!"

"As if I could!" he said, "I—why—I think you're *wonderful!*" he repeated, failing to find better words to express his admiration. "I think you are the kind of girl I want for a real friend. I've been thinking a lot about what you said about God passing on everything before it gets to us. Why, how could I misjudge you after that? You've done a lot for me. Not just introducing me to the store; though I'm grateful for that of course, but you—why you gave me back a kind of decent assurance and faith in Somebody, Something, God I suppose. I almost lost it when things began to happen. And then I saw that you, who have lost so many more things than I have, were standing by and believing in Him and it kind of made me think, and I've been lots happier since. I don't know that I understand things any better, but I somehow *feel* better. You know at college almost nobody believed anything much. Besides, you made me see myself."

"How do you mean, see yourself?" asked Natalie wonderingly.

"Well, you made me see that I had been kind of high-hat. I may as well call it by its right name. You made me see that I had really been a conceited snob, and God, if there is a God who cares about such things, probably had to hand me out all this to show me before I got too hard boiled."

"Well," said Natalie with a little bit of a laugh in her voice, "I can see you're just what I've always thought you were, and—I'm so glad. I hate to be disappointed in people. It's been just beautiful to have you speak out and be so frank with me, and I can't tell you how nice it is to have you friendly. I've been awfully lonesome ever since I came to this town to live. And I'm so glad you haven't thought me forward or anything."

"Well, I'm awfully glad I've found you, and I hope we are going to be wonderful friends. What are you doing to-night? Could I see you somewhere? I'd like to talk to you more about this. I've been all tangled up and you seem to understand me."

"Why," Natalie hesitated, "this is my night to go to the Bible School—if Mother is well enough for me to leave."

"Couldn't I go with you? Couldn't I take care of you? I don't like to have you going around the streets in the dark with a fellow like that tagging after you. May I come for you? What time?"

"Oh, would you go there? You'd like it I'm sure. The man I told you about speaks to-night. It's to be at eight o'clock. But I hate to have you feel you must take your time looking after me. Maybe your people will not like it."

"Why not?" asked Chris looking down at her sweet eyes.

"I'm not in your social class you know," she said gravely.

"Neither am I any more," said Chris quickly and laughed, suddenly realizing that the fact did not hurt him as it had. Somehow there seemed a bond in the fact that they could both laugh over this.

They had come to her door now and she reached out to take her bundles. Quite a staggering load she had dared that night because she had been sure that he had gone home, and he would not feel he had to carry them. But he did not surrender them.

"These are too many for you to lift. Mayn't I come in and put them away for you? That's potatoes, that sack, I know the feel of them after filling nine million bags of them more or less to-day. You shouldn't attempt to carry loads like that. A girl isn't strong enough. That's a man's job."

"Oh, I'm quite strong," laughed Natalie, and tried once more to take them.

"No, please, I'm taking them in, if you don't mind," insisted Chris.

Natalie had a quick vision of her mother in a big apron getting supper, Janice setting the table, horrified expressions perhaps on their faces, and her cheeks flamed scarlet in the dark to think that now her mother would worry again; but there was something in Chris's cultured pleasant voice that made it necessary for her to surrender, and with a quick prayer that all might be well within she threw open the door into the tiny hall.

Mrs. Halsey was just taking a lovely bread pudding out of the oven, crisp and brown on the top, and the spicy odor of cinnamon reached out to the hall fragrantly to the hungry boy.

"My that smells good!" he said as he strode through the hall into the tiny kitchen at the end where the door stood wide open. He walked straight over to the clean kitchen table and deposited his bundles, then turned toward the astonished mother, sweeping off his cap.

"Good evening!" he said with a courteous grin, "You don't know me. I'm just the delivery boy from the chain store. I hope you don't mind my lack of ceremony. I had to lay these down before I could take off my hat."

"Mother, this is Chris Walton," said Natalie appearing behind him with shining eyes, very red cheeks, and a belated introduction.

Mrs. Halsey arose to the occasion beautifully, almost cordially.

"You've been very kind," she said studying the engaging face of the young man searchingly. "I've told Natalie she shouldn't bring so much at once, and she ought not to impose on your good nature."

"Oh, that's nothing," said Chris with a disarming smile. "I live near here you know, and I'm glad to be of use. How cozy you look here. Is that the pudding that smells so good? It certainly smells good enough to eat."

"Won't you stay and help us eat it?" asked the mother smiling cordially.

"Oh, I wish I could, but you see I've got the butter for supper in my pocket, and I expect Mother is flattening her nose against the window pane this very instant watching for me. Sorry. That looks like a real pudding and I'd like to sample it. Perhaps you'll ask me again sometime?"

"Why of course," said Mrs. Halsey. "If you really care to come."

"That's settled then," said Chris turning to Natalie. "There, Natalie, don't you forget to fix that up soon. If you do I'll have to remind you. Now, I must hurry or I'll get a good scolding for not bringing the butter sooner. I'll be back to go to that school with you, Natalie—at seven thirty, did you say? Or is that time enough?"

"Why, it really isn't necessary to start before quarter of eight. It's only a short distance you know," said Natalie, not daring to look at her mother.

"I suppose you've forgotten me entirely," said Janice suddenly appearing in the front room doorway, algebra and pencil in her hand, and her curly hair tossed up in a very little-girl way.

Chris whirled, and looked at her bewildered.

"This is my sister Janice," explained Natalie. "I guess you never saw her before."

"You're not by any chance the little girl with the red tam that I used to draw to school on her sled my last year in High School, are you? Those look like her eyes."

"The very same," said Janice dimpling. "It's several years since I've had a ride on a sled, or anything else for the matter of that."

"Sorry I haven't a bus to take you out in, but I don't even own a wheelbarrow any more. But say, you've grown up fast! I suppose you're in High School now. My, doesn't that make us seem ancient, Natalie? And it only seems yesterday that I took you on your sled to school. Well, I must run along or this butter will melt. See you later."

And Chris hurried away. But as he rounded the corner into the avenue he noticed a slow moving figure, in the shadow on the opposite side of the road, pausing now and then to look furtively up and down the street either way, and he was glad he had decided to go with Natalie to Bible School.

It was Janice that brought the question to debate as the door closed behind him.

"How did that happen, Natalie? I thought you had eschewed the society of gentlemen forevermore and were going to hold Mother's hand."

"Oh, Janice, you make me tired!" said Natalie nervously. "It wasn't my fault. I waited late so he would be gone because I wanted to bring home those lovely potatoes before they were all sold to-morrow, and when I came out the door there he was outside. He hadn't gone at all. I tried to make him understand I could carry my own packages but it wasn't any use. He even was almost offended at me, said he wouldn't bother me if I really was annoyed by him, so there was nothing else to do but let him come. And I can't help it that he is going to Bible School, can I? It was entirely his own idea."

Mrs. Halsey looked at her usually placid daughter in surprise.

"Why, Natalie dear, I never meant to have you feel that way about it," she said anxiously, "I'm sorry. Please forget it, daughter. It was just that I couldn't bear to have you looked down upon by a rich man's son, or get interested in someone who might be beneath you, morally or spiritually, or who might show you attention that would make you care too much when he meant nothing but trifling. But dear, I see I should have trusted you. He seems a very nice boy, and most humble, not a bit spoiled by his wealth."

"But he isn't wealthy any more, Mother," said Natalie earnestly. "They're living over on Sullivan Street near the railroad, next to the woman who used to wash for them. They have given up everything they had and are as poor as we are, I guess, from what I hear."

"Well, dear. I was wrong to judge anyone by money or position. I liked him very much in that brief minute or two, and if you want to ask him here to our plain little home do just as you think best. He'll be welcome with me. Only guard your heart, my precious girl, and don't let it go dreaming. You're my wonderful girl you know, and I can't bear to think that anything should hurt you."

Natalie turned away and pressed her hand against her hot cheeks, as she suddenly remembered the genuine tone in which Chris had said:

"I think you are *wonderful*, you know."

Then Janice, eyeing her sharply, began to chant in a comical tone,

> *"You may go and nibble, nibble, nibble,*
> *At the cheese, cheese, cheese,*
> *Little mouse you may nibble*
> *If you please, please, please,*
> *But be careful little mouse,*
> *Of the cunning little house,*
> *For you may some day find out*
> *That it's a trap, trap, trap!"*

Janice had a sweet clear voice with a mocking resonance in it, and the words rang out comically through the kitchen. Natalie almost on the verge of tears suddenly sat down in a chair and began to laugh hysterically as Janice's soprano rose in an improvised chorus:

*"Oh, my cunning little mouse,*
*Oh, my darling little mouse,*
*Oh, you wonderful, wonderful, wonderful little mouse!"*

Then Natalie suddenly straightened up and looked soberly at her mother and sister.

"Look here, you two dears. You've got to stop this now, once and for all. I just won't be teased this way. I haven't any idea of throwing my heart out in the street for every young man to trample over, and I guess when a girl trusts her life to the Lord for leading He isn't going to let her go the wrong way and give her thoughts to the wrong one is He? Chris is a nice boy and of course I like to have him be polite and kind to me. But I haven't any funny notions and you needn't think I have. If the Lord has someone for me to fall in love with some day He'll likely show me without a question when the time comes, but at present I'm just a girl, and when anybody is friendly, and seems to have right ideas of things I don't know why I shouldn't be friendly with them to a certain extent without having to pass through the inquisition. Now, if you don't both think I'm right about that I'll go upstairs and stay there and when Chris comes back you can send him away and give him any excuse you like for my not going with him. But I won't stand for all these anxieties and fears any longer. It takes the joy out of life. If you don't want me to speak to him I won't, but I don't want to hear any more about it."

"The worm has turned!" said Janice solemnly, into the silence that followed Natalie's outbreak, and then suddenly they all broke down and laughed together.

Finally the mother came and put her arms around Natalie and kissed her softly.

"There, dearie," she said, "you're perfectly right. I had no idea we were persecuting you so. Forgive it, precious. And I'll tell you this. He's a fine nice boy. I can see that at the start. And if you can help him to know the Lord Jesus it will be a great thing. I'm with you. And I know I can trust you every step of the way. It's a great thing when a mother can say that of her child. Now, quiet down, precious, and let's have supper. It's getting late."

"And so am I with you," proclaimed Janice. "I'm so much with you that I'm going to study my algebra this evening and not go to Bible School till next week. There! How is that for sacrifice?"

Natalie stopped short in the middle of the kitchen with her hat in her hand.

"Indeed, you'll do no such thing!" she declared. "I'll help you with your algebra after we come home. But I'm determined you shall start in this class right at the beginning of the first lesson. We're going to take up the book of Hebrews, and its important to hear the introduction or you won't get the same interest. If you stay at home I shall stay too."

"All right, Captain! I'll go then," said Janice gaily. "I want to sacrifice myself in any way possible to keep peace in this household."

Then Natalie turned upon her laughing, and the two girls chased each other round and round from kitchen to living room, to hall and back to kitchen again in a gale of laughter, till they suddenly realized that their mother was doing all the work, and dropped their nonsense to help put the dinner on the table.

There was a pleasant excitement on them all as they ate. It was a new thing for the girls to be going out with a young man. Even Janice, scarcely more than a little girl, felt greatly elated, and the mother seemed as pleased as any of them.

"You'd better put on your other dress, Natalie," said her mother, as they began to gather up the dishes. "You run up and dress and I can do these few dishes just as well as not."

"No," said Natalie determinedly. "I'm not dolling up just because a boy I used to go to school with is going along. If he doesn't like me the way I am he needn't go. It's a plain school, and people don't dress up to go there. I'm going to do these dishes. You got dinner, and I can see you're tired."

In the end they all did the dishes, the mother sitting down and wiping the silver, and they were done in a trice, and then Natalie did change her blouse and wear her Sunday hat, but neither of them said anything about it. Indeed there wasn't time, for they could hear Chris's quick crisp step on the walk, and his clear whistle, and then came the sound of his knock on the door.

"Seems like being regular people, doesn't it?" said Janice softly under her breath as she started for the door. "The Halsey family is going out among 'em!"

And as they started off happily with their escort Mrs. Halsey sighed half sadly, to think that a simple little pleasure like going out to a religious meeting could bring such delight! They were dear girls! How little real youthful pleasure they had had in their lives! If their father had only lived—!

Then she slipped up to her room and knelt a long time by her bed asking for wisdom to guide and guard her children aright, wisdom that should show her distinctly, step by step, what the Lord would have her do, and help her not to get her own will in the way of the Lord's leading.

CHRIS went to the Bible School that night and heard a wonderful talk from a man who spoke as if he were personally acquainted with Jesus Christ, had talked to Him face to face, and received his instructions from a Bible that seemed to be vivid and real, not just mystical sayings mysteriously handed down from dim uncertain ages almost forgotten. Chris was deeply stirred.

Under this magical teacher, words, phrases, even verses and chapters with which he had had a verbal acquaintance since his childhood, suddenly sprang into new, wonderful meaning. It seemed like witch work. He looked around on the earnest company who were listening, Bibles and note books open on their laps, their eyes fixed on the speaker. There wasn't one among them who had the look of a doubter. Their faces seemed almost illumined with inner light. And when he glanced at Natalie she had the same rapt look. Even young Janice seemed deeply engrossed.

How did this man find out all these wonderful things? Were they merely interpretations? But no, he did not seem to be twisting the words, for he read them as they were printed. Natalie had found the place and handed him a Bible. He could follow along, and lo, the story with which he was familiar was there, and yet meant as clearly as print just what the teacher said it meant. That was entirely obvious. And all just because the teacher had explained the meaning of a Greek word, and made them turn to several other references.

The teacher said more than once that scripture must be interpreted by itself, comparing scripture with scripture, and it certainly was wonderful how it worked out and made things clear. Why, some of the passages that were read he had learned by heart when he was a child in the primary class, but nobody ever took the trouble to make them plain to him, and they had never meant a thing in his mind except a lot of words.

He learned for the first time, just in casual reference that the Bible was written according to a marvelous numerical structure. Each book and verse and even each word was worked out mathematically and so perfectly, that it was possible to distinguish between two copies of ancient manuscripts that differed slightly, and identify the original, because the incorrect one would not conform to the numerical structure. He learned that this could only be proved and studied in the Hebrew and Greek, and a sudden desire to study those languages was born in him. He would like to be able to prove that thing. If it was true it upset all the doubts of his college professors; because the teacher went on to state that no scholar had been able to write a single paragraph in imitation of this numerical structure and make good sense out of it; that no other book had as yet been found to be written in this way; that this same law of numbers governs every department of creation; the conclusion being that the God who was the Creator of the earth is also the Author of the Book.

He caught a slight vision of the symbolism all through the Bible, of the significance of numbers, of the significance of the meaning of every proper name in the Bible. He heard references to dispensational truth that made clear as day sentences that he had always considered vague.

When the lesson finally closed with a prayer that left its imprint on his heart, he found that he was distinctly sorry it was over. It seemed as if the talk had been only about ten minutes in length, but when he looked at his watch he found it had been a full hour in duration. He would be glad if there were to be another lesson immediately following. He would have enjoyed asking a lot of questions, but he would sooner have cut off a small piece of his tongue than own to it.

The teacher stood at the door as they went out, took Chris's hand in a warm quick grip and called him brother, with a sweet bright look that seemed when he thought of it afterward like lightning, coming from a strong place filled with both joy and sorrow.

When they were out in the night again a silence fell upon the three. At last Janice spoke:

"I think he's wonderful, don't you, Natalie?"

"It's a wonderful book we're studying," said Natalie thoughtfully. "And he knows it well."

"There's one thing I'd like to know," said Chris, more as if he were thinking aloud, than really expecting to be answered. "He kept talking about 'saved ones.' What did he mean? *Who* did he mean? How could anybody tell whether they were saved or not?"

"Oh," breathed Natalie earnestly. "You can, of course! Don't you know whether you're saved?"

"Why, no," said Chris, "Of course not. Nobody knows about that till after they're dead, do they? And anyhow, what does it mean, saved from what?"

"Why, saved from the consequences of sin, which is death."

"I've never felt that I was such a great sinner," said Chris just the least bit loftily.

Natalie was silent a moment, then she lifted her head bravely. "We're all great sinners," she stated quietly.

"I don't see that," said Chris stubbornly, "what have you done that's so awful? What have I? Of course little things. But I've always tried to live a pretty decent life."

"Of course the great sin, the only sin, after all, that is terrible, is not believing in Him. Rejecting Him when He did so much for us. The Bible says that in God's sight 'All have sinned and come short of the glory of God.'"

"Of course I've heard that line all my life, but down in my heart I never did see why so much emphasis was put on sin. Most respectable people are pretty good livers. I never had any real desire to be bad. I can't really feel that I'm a great sinner and I don't see why I should try."

Natalie was praying silently that she might be given the right answer, and now she said half shyly:

"People never do feel they are sinners till they've had a vision of Jesus, do they? When you see what He is then you begin to know how far short you fall."

"Oh!" said Chris blankly. Then after a moment, "How could you do that? He isn't here. You can't see a person that isn't here."

"Yes, you can. You can find Him in His Word. And you can find Him in prayer. The Holy Spirit has promised to reveal Him to us if we ask Him. But you've got to come believing. Belief is the key that unlocks the Word and makes us see things that we could not understand without it."

Chris looked at her wonderingly.

"How could one believe something they *didn't* believe? Something they were not convinced was true?"

"Belief is an act of the will," said Natalie, "not an intellectual conviction. It is something you deliberately will to do. It is taking God at His word and letting Him prove to you that what He promises is true. That is the way it was put in Bible School the other night, and I've proved it is true."

*"You* have?" he eyed her curiously in the soft darkness of the street.

"Oh, yes! Ever since I was saved."

"There it is again," said Chris perplexedly, "you say it just the way he did to-night, as if it were some sort of charm. What does it mean? How do you get that way? What do you have to do?"

"Oh, you don't have to *do* anything. Just accept it. Just believe it. Salvation is a free gift, and you've only to take it. The moment you accept it you are saved, and nothing, not *anything* can take you out of His hand, for you are His, and from that time forth you are under His care, and He says He is able to present you *faultless* before the presence of His glory without spot or wrinkle or any such thing. That's not because *you* are without fault. That's because *He* is faultless, and because He has given us a right to wear *His righteousness*. It is only through His righteousness that we could be faultless." Natalie was talking earnestly now, herself filled with wonder that she had been given opportunity to say these things.

"But I don't quite understand," said Chris. "How does that make you know you are saved, just to accept a thing? Just to believe?"

"Why," said Natalie thoughtfully, praying that she might be led to the right words that would bring light to the questioner, "if you were a prisoner, condemned to die, and you were told that someone else had taken the death penalty for you and you might go free, all that would be left for you to do would be to accept his death for yours, to believe what you were told. He has said that the minute you accept His grace and believe His word you are born again, and are one of His saved ones. He also says: 'He that believeth *hath* everlasting life, and *shall not* come into condemnation, but *is passed* from death unto life.'"

"But I don't just see how believing a thing could make any difference in the way you feel."

"Well, you couldn't see, because belief is the thing that makes it possible for you to see. It is the key that unlocks the mystery, and you can't find out until you try it yourself. Nobody can make you see it. You have to take that key of belief and unlock it for yourself. You do it in other things. Why not trust God as well as men? Suppose you are very much in need of something at the store and you ask the manager about it and he says he'll get it right away and then you don't worry about it any more. You just trust it to him. Yet you don't really *know* he will do it. You haven't *proved* him perhaps, but you take it for granted he will keep his word. You will to believe him till he has disproved himself. Why not take God at His word?"

Chris was silent, pondering. At last he said:

"But I'm a church member, you know. Doesn't that make it all right?"

"No," said Natalie sadly. "He didn't say 'If you join the church you are saved,—passed from death unto life.' He said 'He that believeth.'"

They had reached the house now and were pausing at the door.

"Won't you come in?" asked Natalie shyly, wondering if her mother would approve of her asking him.

"No," said Chris, "it's getting late and you and I have

to be up early. But—I'd like to know more about this. We'll talk about it another time. Perhaps I'll join that class. I like that bird. He's sincere, you can see that. Well, good night!" and he left them almost abruptly.

"Queer," he said to himself as he walked home, "I never knew she was a girl like that! How different she is from the other girls I used to know in school. Fancy any of them talking about how to be saved, or caring about it!"

He kept asking himself why he hadn't known this lovely girl before? Why hadn't he sought her out and taken her to places instead of some of the fool girls he used to go with?

Oh, those other girls weren't all silly girls of course. Janie Anderson and Marguerite Manning, and Roxana White were sensible bright fine girls. He had sometimes taken them here and there. But no girl had ever so stirred him as this sweet spirit who had sat by him to-night listening to that most unusual message. He realized that much of the pleasure of the evening had come from watching her lovely earnest face as she listened.

As he swung up to his own door he told himself that a strong tie had been welded between that girl and himself that evening. Of course they were both young, and it was not time yet to think of more serious things, but his heart felt that the friendship with Natalie Halsey had come into his life to stay. Here was a character with something more to it than froth. Something more even than a good education, pleasant manners, and a desire to please. Life had early sifted her and tested her. Her face bore the marks of experience that had not hardened her, but brought a lovely peace upon her brow and a charming light in her eyes. He felt a wistful longing to understand and have the same secret that she possessed.

13

THE days that followed were full of hard work, but it was somehow very pleasant work to Chris. The fellows in the store were still a little belligerent, jealous of any word the manager spoke to him, ready to criticize and sneer behind his back. But there was always the boss now, liking him and saying nice things occasionally about his work, for he was selling now with the rest and understood the stock as well as anyone. And there was always Natalie to watch furtively when a moment of leisure came, Natalie in her little glass cage, making change with her white fingers, smiling to the women customers, gravely courteous to the men, sending the ghost of a little bright flash from her eyes to him across the store now and then when no one would be watching.

They were very careful not to let their friendship be known. It seemed too indefinite, almost too sacred to be dragged through the store, and joked about as it inevitably would have been if it had become known. None of their fellow employees knew even that Natalie had recommended Chris, he discovered. She went her quiet way among them, smiling shyly to each one, but holding aloof. Even the manager spoke most respectfully to her, and they all called her Miss Halsey, not Natalie.

Every night Chris lingered in some place agreed upon and they walked home together, he carrying whatever bundles she had, but they managed their meetings around the corner, or after the others had left. The tramp-man who had troubled their first acquaintance seemed to have disappeared. He stood no longer at the corner of the street mornings when Natalie started out and she was greatly relieved.

The weeks went swiftly by.

"Mother, I think Chris has a girl," said Elise one evening when they were waiting for Chris to come to dinner. Sometimes he was unaccountably later than need be.

"Oh!" said his mother looking up a little anxiously, "Do you think so? I—suppose—he—would—some-time, but—he seems so young."

"He's no younger than I was when I fell in love with you, Mother," said her elderly lover looking up unexpectedly from his paper.

"Well, that was different," said Mother smiling. "You were—I was—that is—"

"Exactly so," said Father with a twinkle. "I was just thinking that myself."

"What makes you think he has a girl, Elise?" asked her mother.

"Well, I've seen him twice walking with her, very slowly when I went down for Daddy's paper. It's just after the store closes."

"Oh, I hope it's not Anna Peters," said the mother with quick apprehension in her voice.

"No, it's not Anna," said the sister triumphantly. "Chris can't bear her. He says she's bold."

"She is!" agreed the mother.

"It's a girl around here," announced Elise discreetly.

"Around *here!*" there was consternation in the mother's voice.

"Yes, I think she lives over on Cromar Street. I thought I heard his voice the other night as I was crossing at the corner. If it's the house where he was standing her sister is in my class in school. And she used to be in Chris's class in High School."

"Who is she?"

"She is one of the Halsey girls. I think her name is Natalie. Her sister is Janice Halsey. Janice seems nice, only we don't any of us know her very well. She always has to hurry home. Her mother's been sick. Janice wears made-over dresses."

"That's nothing against her," said the mother sharply. Her own daughter would probably come to that very soon.

"Well, she's pretty, but the girls don't invite her much."

"Better get acquainted, daughter, and bring her around," suggested Father. "It would be nice to know what the family are like. Of course there may be nothing serious in carrying bundles. Chris is a gentleman, and it would be natural to walk with one who lived near here, but Mother, if Chris is getting acquainted with someone you'd better find out who she is and invite her here. That will make a friendship safe and sane you know. Chris is young, and of course the girls have always liked him. It's natural he'll want friends."

"I will," said Mother with a sigh; and just then Chris came whistling up on the porch, his face the picture of happiness.

The next afternoon as she was coming down the high school steps Elise caught sight of Janice Halsey just turning out of the school pavement into the street and called to her.

"Janice! Janice Halsey! Oh, I say, Janice, wait for me a minute!" she called hurrying down the steps and after her swift as a swallow.

Janice paused in surprise. She was accustomed to hurrying away as soon as school closed and not lingering to talk with the girls. Her mother had needed her for so long that it had become second nature with her, even when the need for haste was not quite so urgent. And the girls had fallen into the habit of not counting her in things when they planned for parties and festivities.

"Oh, she wouldn't come!" someone would say if ever her name was mentioned by some newcomer in school. "She has to work or something. She's always in a hurry!" and they let it go at that. So Janice, who used to play with them down in the Primary grades, and knew them all, was no more one of them than her sister had been when she was in High School.

So now she stood and waited, gravely surprised, her eyes speculative. What could Elise Walton want of her? Only some message from the teacher probably, maybe about the essay she was to write for the Friday class. Or perhaps it was to tell her of the class banquet; they always went through the gesture of inviting her to it, though they knew she never accepted because she hadn't the two dollars a plate that it cost.

She stood poised, half impatient, and waited until Elise caught up with her, breathless and friendly, with a real smile. She had always admired Elise from afar, especially had she admired her clothes. They were always so lovely, so exquisite, so perfect in every detail, with so many little touches of distinction about them, and Janice delighted to get a closer view of them that she might sometimes copy a little feature in her own made-over garments.

"I wondered," panted Elise, as she fell into step with Janice just as if they had always been close friends, "if you wouldn't take pity on me and explain that algebra problem that you did on the board this morning. You did it so beautifully, and so quickly, but the period was over almost as you finished and I didn't have time to see what you did. Where did you get that quotient? I simply can't figure it out. I've been working for the last ten minutes over it. You see, there's another almost like it in our lesson for to-morrow."

"Why of course I'll show you," said Janice in surprise. "But you are always quicker at algebra than I am. You wouldn't have any trouble getting it if you just took a little time."

"But I haven't the time," said Elise rather breathlessly. "You see," she laughed half shamedly, "I'm in a hurry to-day because Mother and I are going to try papering a room. We've never done one before and I don't know how it will come out but I'm so excited about it I don't know what to do. You see it's my brother's room and we want to surprise him with it. Did you ever do any paper hanging?"

"I certainly have," smiled Janice in a superior way. "We always do ours. My sister is a clipper at it. She can put it on as smooth as the skin on your face. Only she's busy all day now. She works in the chain store up on the avenue."

"Oh!" said Elise with a bit of a gasp at the thought. "Which sister is that?"

"I haven't but one sister," said Janice. "There are only three of us, Mother and Natalie and myself, since Father died."

"Oh, I didn't know your father died," said Elise

sympathetically. "How hard that must have been. My father almost died a few weeks ago. We didn't know for days and days whether he was going to get well or not."

"Yes, I know," said Janice sympathetically. "Mother read about it in the papers. You know, he's the president of our bank, and we were interested—" then she stopped suddenly and realized that was something she should not have spoken about.

"Oh," said Elise with sudden trouble in her eyes. "Were you among the people who lost all their money through us? Oh, I'm so sorry—!"

"Don't worry," said Janice trying to laugh it off gaily. "We didn't have much there to lose. Mother had just had to draw almost all of it out to make the last payment on our house."

"How fortunate!" said the other girl. "But Father says he hopes everybody is going to get back all they lost in a little while. As soon as he gets stronger he's going to try and do something about it, I don't know what. But oh, I hope you'll get all yours soon."

"Oh, I don't believe there was enough there to matter," laughed Janice again, wishing she hadn't said anything about it. "What's this about the problem? Do you mean the one about the pumps? Why, you divide the quotient by nine, don't you see?" and Janice opened her book and the two girls walked slowly along with their heads together over the algebra.

"Oh, yes, of course, how stupid of me!" said Elise at last. "My, I'm glad I asked you. Now it won't take me ten minutes to get my work finished for morning and I can go at the papering right away before dark. The man who sold us the paper told us a little about putting it on, but I'm scared to death about the ceiling. He told us to get a new dust brush and smooth it ahead down the middle of a strip of paper, but he warned me it was hard to keep it on, and hard to make it go straight. I'm afraid I shall make a mess of it."

Janice laughed.

"It is hard till you get used to it. The first time I ever put any paper on a ceiling it came down behind my shoulders just as fast as I put it on, and when I got to the end of the strip I was all wound up in it. Oh, I was a mess."

The two girls laughed over this and Elise made a wry face.

"I expect I'll make a mess of the whole thing," she said, "but I've got to try for my mother was going to do it herself and I can't have her getting up on chairs and step ladders and breaking her hip or something. My mother put on some wall-paper once when she was a young married woman."

"Well, mine didn't, because she didn't have to then, they were well off, but she had to later when we lost all our money, and Natalie and I have been brought up to do everything that we could. If we didn't make things we didn't have them. But it's kind of fun to make things and do things like papering, don't you think so?"

"Sometimes," laughed Elise, "I'll tell you better when I get this paper on the wall. I wish you could come in and sort of coach me."

"I wish I could," said Janice wistfully, "but I've got to hurry right home. Mother has been doing some fine sewing for a woman and she wants it before five o'clock, so I must take it. But if there's anything else I can do to help later I'd love to."

"Thank you," said Elise, "I may call on you yet. By the way, why don't you come over and see me? We're rather near neighbors, aren't we?"

"Yes, we are," said Janice consciously, as if she had considered the matter before, but hadn't expected it to be recognized. "I'd love to sometime, if I can get the time. You see—well, we're pretty busy, all of us, most of the time. Since my sister got the position in the chain store I have to take her place getting dinner and doing a good deal of the housework, because Mother has been sick and she really isn't able to do the housework and her sewing too, and we really need the money from her sewing."

"Well, we're busy at our home too," said Elise frankly. "I've got a job taking care of kids three times a week, so now I am proud to say I rank in the laboring class too. I guess I've been pretty useless most of my life, but I'm trying to make up for it now as well as I can. You know you don't realize when you don't have to what a difference it makes. But honestly, I think it's kind of fun."

Janice looked grave.

"Well," she said sadly, "it's fun sometimes of course to put up with things and try and make ends meet, but when someone you love is very sick and there isn't enough money to get the fruit and things they ought to have, and when someone dies, and things all get snarled up it isn't so much fun."

Elise looked at her speculatively.

"I like you," she said suddenly, "I wish we could be friends. I don't know why we haven't been before."

"I've always liked you," said Janice grinning, "but I never had time for being friends with anybody. It's nice to know you want to be friends though, and I'd love it."

"Well, let's go to school to-morrow together," proposed Elise. "What time do you start? I'll wait in the house till I see you pass our corner."

"All right!" said Janice with dancing eyes, "I'd love that. I've never had anybody to walk to school with since Natalie finished High School."

"Well, you have now," said Elise reaching out impulsively and squeezing Janice's hand. "It's going to be nice. I'm glad!"

The two girls parted happily and Janice hurried home eagerly.

"Mother, what do you think?" she cried as she burst into the house. "Elise Walton ran after me and asked me to help her with her algebra, and she wants to be friends. Do you suppose her brother made her do that? She was really pleasant and lovely about it, as if she meant it."

"Then I wouldn't question it, dear," said her mother looking up wearily from her sewing. "Did you like her?"

"Oh, she was lovely," said Janice. "And Mother, she isn't the least bit snobbish. She and her mother are going to paper a room this afternoon. She says her mother used to do it when she was first married. I was telling her about putting on ceilings, how careful you had to be."

Mrs. Halsey looked up surprised.

"Are they really as hard pressed as that, I wonder?" she said. "I've heard Mr. Walton has been most honorable about giving up his property, but I did not suppose it would really bring them down to doing such things for themselves. It must be very hard for them." Then after a moment of thought,

"I wonder if they have a roller to make the seams smooth? Suppose you take ours with you and go around that way when you take Mrs. Graves' night dresses home. It certainly would be easier for them to have one, and if they own one it can't do any harm to offer a little neighborliness."

So Janice hunted up the little roller they used in their paperhanging and started joyously on her errand.

Elise had found her mother up in the room they were to paper, wearing an old dress, with her sleeves rolled up and a pretty good imitation of a scaffolding rigged up with the ironing board, the kitchen table and two chairs.

She had just finished cutting the last length of ceiling paper as Elise burst into the room.

"Mother! Where are you? You haven't broken your promise and begun, have you? Oh, Mother! You carried up that kitchen table all by yourself!" she cried.

"No, I didn't. Chris ran home a little while ago to get his overcoat instead of his sweater. The store is sending him in town on an errand and he was afraid he would be cold. He brought the table up for me. And go look in my room and see what a nice pasting table I've got fixed up with the two cutting tables and some boards I found in the cellar. No, I didn't carry them up either. I got that little Jimmy next door to bring them for me when he came home at noon for his lunch, and I gave him ten cents and a red apple to pay for doing it. Hurry up and let's get at this. The paste is all ready."

While Elise changed into an old dress she talked.

"Well, Mother dear, I scraped up a friendship with the sister of Chris's girl," she announced, as she slipped out of her pretty school dress.

"Oh, my dear! I don't know that I would call any one Chris's girl on so slight a foundation. Surely if she meant anything special to Chris he would say something about it to your father and me."

"I wonder!" said Elise meditatively.

"I'm quite sure he would," said the mother as if she wished to convince herself.

"Well, anyhow, I liked her a lot, the sister I mean," said Elise. "I guess she's been lonely. She didn't say so, but she seemed very glad that I wanted to be friends."

"Is she—refined, dear? I don't mean, of course, that we should despise her if she isn't—but—well, you know what I mean. I wouldn't like Chris to be interested in bold forward girls,—or coarse ones."

"She's not any of those things, Mother. Really she's

nice. I'm sure you would call her refined. She has a low sweet voice, and a way of looking straight at you, quietly, and waiting for you to speak instead of rushing in as if she knew it all."

"Well, that sounds good. But you don't know about the other sister, do you? This one is the youngest. The other one may be different."

"Yes, I found out about the other one. I don't suppose you'll like it, but—well—she works in the chain store!"

The mother turned around and faced her daughter, an anxious thoughtful look upon her face.

"You don't say!" she said perplexed. "Of course that might explain the bundles. Chris may be only showing kindness to a fellow workman. But—it is so easy for people thrown together that way, to get interested in each other when they're not truly congenial. I should hate to have Chris spoil his life by getting attached to a common girl. But still, it does seem as if Chris would have sense about it. I am sure he has fine ideals."

"Of course, Mother. He has. I wouldn't worry. And—it may not be anything but a little kindness as you say. I don't see, Motherie, why you can't just trust things like that to God. You trust a lot of other things just as big."

Mrs. Walton looked at her daughter with a startled glance. Elise was not one to speak much of God. She wondered if she had been giving a poor witness.

"I suppose I should," she said with a smile, "one forgets at times when a new peril looms that life is not all in our own hands to plan for. Elise, dear, wasn't that a knock at the door? Can you run down, or shall I?"

But Elise was already on her way.

She opened the door and there stood Janice with the little roller.

"Mother thought you might not have a roller and

would like to use ours," she said half shy again before this girl whom she had held in awe so many years.

"Oh, how wonderful! It was darling of you to think of it. No, of course we never even knew there was such a tool. How do you use it? Won't you come in just a minute and show me? Come upstairs and meet my mother. She'd love it. No, I won't keep you but a second, but I do want you to know my mother, and then you can show us how to use this cute thing."

So, much against her will Janice consented to go upstairs.

"It's Janice Halsey, Mother," called Elise as they mounted the high narrow stairs. "She's brought us the darlingest little roller to use on the seams of the paper. Wasn't that lovely? Her mother sent it over."

"Oh, a roller!" said Mrs. Walton coming cordially to the head of the stairs. "How nice! I used to have one long years ago. I don't know what became of it. Janice Halsey, I'm glad to meet you, and it was very kind of you to be so thoughtful for us. Won't you thank your mother for me?"

Janice didn't stay but a minute or two, and when she was gone Elise came back and got to work in earnest.

"Didn't you like her, Mother?" she asked as she watched her mother looking out the window after the departing Janice.

"Yes," said the mother turning with satisfaction from the window, "very much. Of course one can't judge a person in a minute or two, but she seems well bred. I was watching her walk. She moves with a natural grace. Now that Anna Peters swags. She can't take a step without swagging, and when she stands with her slinky coats wrapped around her hips she looks like a half a hoop. One wonders why her legs don't break off somewhere around the knees with the balance of her body utterly destroyed as it is. And she goes around smoking on the street and in her car. I've seen her. She's a bold huzzy!"

Elise laughed gaily.

"Oh, Motherie, you're so funny when you don't like someone. Anna Peters does that on purpose. It's the fashion, Mums, to stand that way, all slunk back."

"Well, don't you ever let me catch you standing that way!" said her mother firmly. "Now this little Janice is a lady. She must have had a well bred mother."

"Janice says her mother never used to have to work," said Elise thoughtfully. "Isn't it queer how people and circumstances just change when they get ready, and you can't do anything about it? You just have to do the best you can?"

"I suppose, dear, that God plans it all," said her mother with a sweet trustfulness.

"Well, if you believe that, why do you ever worry, Motherie?"

Mrs. Walton was silent a moment again and then gave her daughter a sweet smile.

"I oughtn't ever to, ought I?" she said. "Well, I don't mean to, but sometimes I just forget what a great God we have. Now, dear, shall we get to work? I'm quite pleased to have you cultivate that sweet child, and someday perhaps we'll go and see the mother. I just hope the older sister is as possible."

It was only a few days later that a tall rough-looking man came into the store and bought a pound of cheese and a box of crackers.

Chris waited upon him and noticed a long jagged scar across one cheek. He noticed also that he walked about the store, stared at the cash window a good deal, and waited till Natalie was at liberty. Then he pushed his check and the money in, and Chris saw his lips move in a remark, and twist in an ugly familiar laugh. Chris felt his anger rise, but he had to turn to his next customer, a fussy old lady who wanted to inspect every orange he put in the bag for her. When he looked up the man was just sauntering out of the door, with a leer and a grin back at Natalie who had looked away from the door with deep annoyance in her eyes. Chris wondered what was familiar about the sag of his shoulders as he went away, and it was not until later in the day that it recurred to him and he thought about the bum on the street corner, and mentally compared the two. Had that fellow turned up again and hunted out Natalie to annoy her? He felt an undercurrent of worry all the afternoon.

It was a busy day and Chris had no time to think much.

The manager let most of the men go early that night.

Chris was down cellar piling up a lot of boxes that had been thrown downstairs in a hurry that afternoon. He did not like his orderly basement to get in a mess for the next morning.

The boss came down the stairs and spoke to him.

"Walton, they're all gone but Miss Halsey and I think she's almost through. She has three cents too much in her balance sheet and is trying to find out her mistake, but I think it won't take her long. Would you two mind closing up the store to-night? I promised my wife I'd meet her and take her out to-night. Do you mind?"

Chris promised with a smile, proud that he was trusted to close up. The boss usually wouldn't let anybody but himself do that.

He heard the manager say good night to Natalie and go out the door. He put the last box in place, shoved back some of the tins of canned goods that had been disarranged, picked up some scattered excelsior, snapped out the light, and came upstairs.

He was wearing old shoes with soft pliable soles, and his footsteps made no sound as he came. He enjoyed the thought of getting a glimpse of Natalie before she saw him. Her sweet face always filled him with exultation that there could be a girl so lovely and unspoiled.

Then he stepped into the store room and came within sight of the little glass cage where Natalie sat and his blood froze with horror, for there straight within range standing in front of Natalie stood a tall man wearing a small black mask on the upper part of his face, and pointing a revolver straight at her!

14

FOR an instant Chris stood paralyzed with horror. Without stopping to think it out he knew instinctively that Natalie would not be one to give up easily, throw up her hands and hand over her cash register. She would not think of herself, and she would fight to the last hope.

And there wasn't any hope. He could see that this man was a hard one who didn't care what he did. It seemed incredible that this should happen, only half past six in the evening on a street that an hour earlier would have been crowded with passers by, in a store that five short minutes before would have been well protected by a large force of men. Every one of them gone, and he the only one left! Doubtless the bandit knew that, or bandits, for there were probably at least two of them. They must have thought that he was gone too. He had been down cellar for some little time, and the store would seem empty to an inlooker from the street. He must not let them know of his presence till he could first do something to protect Natalie, to protect the cash in the register and safe. He happened to know that there was a larger amount of money than usual in the safe, brought in that afternoon after the bank had closed.

And now Natalie would be required to open that safe, and quickly too. Would she do it? He felt afraid that she might stand out against it. Indeed she seemed to be doing so now.

She was sitting up straight and white in her little glass room, her eyes big and frightened looking into that ugly menacing gun, but she had not put up her hands as she had been told to do.

"Put 'em up, girlie, and dontcha touch that telephone," came the ugly command. "Up with 'em an' you march out here. You gotta open that safe in the back room, and do it good and quick, see? Up with 'em I say! I ain't got time to waste. I'll count three, see? An' ef they ain't up when I gets to three I shoots, see? And when I shoots I *shoots*. I ain't no softie. I don't mind layin' out a little pretty one like you. I shoots ta kill! One!—"

The store was awfully still and Chris felt as if his heart had stopped. It was up to him to do something before it was too late. Could he get out and call for help? He had no weapon. He could not hope to handle a man with a gun single-handed.

"Two!" The word fell like a bullet deep into his heart. Natalie had not stirred. She had not lifted her hands. Her sweet mouth was set firmly, and she was white as death. Oh, there must be something he could do. He glanced around, and saw close at his side a big basket of hard green apples. Could he do it? All those years of his boyhood when he had practiced pitching baseball, came to his mind, but quicker than any thought came an earlier practice to his lips, a practice learned at his mother's knee in babyhood. "Oh, God, help me save her!"

Silently he seized an apple, crouched in the old position and swung his arm. Could he hit that gun and knock it out of the man's hand? And if he did would it perhaps go off and kill Natalie? "Oh, God! Oh, God!" and suddenly he knew that he believed there was a God.

The hard green missile whizzed through the air like a bullet. There was a crash and an explosion, but Chris could not stop to see what had happened. Another apple went whizzing and struck the enemy on the temple. He had started for the door but it dazed him and as he looked back Chris gave him another apple full in the nose, with another in the eyes.

"Oh God! Oh God! Help me!" prayed Chris, in his heart, and aimed another apple, when suddenly to his surprise he saw the man crumple to the floor. Could just apples knock a man out? He plunged across the room and was upon him with a wrestling hold he had learned in high school days. The man struggled and kicked out at him, then smashed a blinding blow across Chris's eyes, so that the room was full of stars, bright hard stars, and his head was swimming, but still he kept his grip on the man's throat. And where was Natalie? She had disappeared from sight. What voice was that he heard? And how did all these people get into the store?

He opened one swollen eye and saw brass buttons. Of course the police headquarters was almost next door, but how did they know to come? They must have heard the report of the gun. Oh, was Natalie killed?

They loosened his hold upon the throat of the bandit, set him upon his feet, wiped the blood from his nose, and patted him on his shoulder.

"Good work, boy!" they said, and he could hear the click of handcuffs on the arms of the man on the floor who was struggling for his breath.

"Where is she?" Chris cried out wildly, his heart bursting with fear.

"Where's who? What? You mean the one that telephoned us? Why, who was she anyway? The cashier?"

They jerked the door of the little glass cage open and there was Natalie lying on the floor in a heap with the telephone in her limp hand and her mouth to the instrument, but she did not stir. She was quite unconscious.

Chris was down on his knees at once, lifting her out as if she had been a baby, staggering up with her in his arms.

"He must have got her after all!" he groaned.

"No such thing!" said a man in the crowd coming closer. "She's just fainted. I seen that gun fall. It went off in the corner quite harmless. I was just coming by the store on my way an' I seen that first apple come flyin' an' hit that guy just as pretty! Man, that was some pitchin'! I couldn't rightly make out what was doing, I thought ta myself the men here was kiddin' each other in the absence of the manager. I thought they was wastin' good apples an' oughtta be reported, till I heard that there gun go off in the corner down by the door, almost next ta me. An' then right away I heard the p'lice whistle, and they come flyin' from headquarters, an' I knowed somethin' was doin', but how'd you get onta it? Somebuddy come an' tell ya?"

"Call came over the wire, 'Chain-store! Hold up!' that was all," said the chief of police shortly, "It was a woman's voice. Guess she done it," and he nodded toward Natalie. "Boys get some water," he ordered sharply. "She's gotta be brought to. She's some brave little girl she is."

Chris laid her gently upon the floor and put water to her lips, took a clean handkerchief from his pocket and bathed her face, and presently she opened her eyes and stared around in amazement on the crowd.

"Oh, are you all right, Chris?" she murmured.

"Sure thing!" grinned Chris in relief. "Don't talk now. Wait. I'm heating you some coffee. There was some left over from what the men had at noon. No, don't get up till I bring it."

More people were gathering now. A woman who occupied the apartment over the drug store across the way said she was sitting at the window watching for her husband's train to come in and had seen the whole thing. She said the store was light enough for her to see the apples come flying across the room and it seemed as if there were a bushel of them.

A small boy who scarcely ever was known to miss a great thrill like that testified that he heard the gun go off and got on the spot while the apples were flying. He said he saw the big guy get hit in the nose and go down.

The confusion quieted down after a few minutes. Chris brought Natalie coffee and made her drink it, and when she was able to sit up they sent her home in a taxi, though she would look after putting her cash register in the safe first, herself.

Chris took her home but insisted that he was coming right back.

"I was put in charge. I think I'll just come back and stay here till I can get the manager on the telephone. He won't likely be back to his house till late this evening, but I'd feel better just to stay here till I get word from him."

He was holding his handkerchief to his bruised cheek now, but he was happy. Boy! he was happy, he told himself, looking across at Natalie who had her hat and coat on now.

"I think I ought to stay too," she protested, "Mr. Foster left me here too, and told me what to do about the money."

"No, Miss Halsey. You gotta get some rest after that bout. You been some brave lady, but it ain't fer a woman to go through them things like you done and then try ta sit up on a stiff hard stool all evenin' till yer boss comes. You go home an' get some rest or you won't be on hand ta-morra, and you'll be needed then, see?" said the natty young policeman who had ordered the taxi.

"Yes, you two done good work," said another policeman coming up. "We been watchin' that there guy fer about three weeks. He's been hangin' around kind o' suspicious like, but we couldn't get nothin' on him, an' now we caught him in the act, with plenty o' witnesses. Course I ain't sure, but he looks ta me like one o' them guys that's got his mug in the rogues' gallery. If so you two done even better than you expected. Don't you worry, lady. We'll stick around an' guard this little old store right careful ta-night. You just take yer rest till ta-morra."

So Chris put Natalie carefully into the taxi, as if she had been a glass vase of priceless value, and climbed joyously in after her.

15

FOR an instant they looked at one another in the darkness, then his hand sought hers and clasped it close.

"Oh, you were *wonder*ful!" said Natalie softly, letting her hand lie happily in his. "I stayed conscious long enough to see the first two apples go straight to the mark, and then I felt myself going down and had just sense enough to grab the telephone and take it with me."

"Thank the great God you are safe!" said Chris, "Safe! Oh, I shall never doubt Him again! I prayed, Natalie! All the time I was firing apples at that sucker I prayed to God to help me!"

"Oh, Chris!" said Natalie bringing her other hand around and putting it over their clasped ones with a caressing motion, and never realizing at all what she did, "that's the *dearest,* best thing of all. I've prayed so much that you might believe!"

"You prayed for me, Natalie?" he asked wonderingly.

"Oh, yes. I've been praying for you ever since the day you talked about getting a raw deal. I'm so glad, so glad, that you've found Him. Why, I'd have been willing to go through much more terrible things to have you come to see that. It's been the dearest wish of my heart."

"Natalie, darling—!" Chris reached over and drew her close to his heart, folding his arms about her reverently, "Oh, you wonderful, beautiful little girl, I love you. I thank God that He has saved you from that devil's gun. Oh, Natalie, I thought he had killed you!" He buried his face on her shoulder, and when she put her hands up caressingly she found there were tears on his cheek.

Natalie laid her face against his then and touched his wet eyelids softly with her lips, and then Chris lifted his head and put his own lips on hers, and such joy went over him as he had never thought to know on earth. Was love like this?

Then suddenly he sat upright again, his arms still about her, and spoke, eagerly, earnestly.

"Natalie, dear,—I suppose I haven't any business to be talking about love—in my position. A mere clerk in a chain store on a starvation salary, with family responsibilities and a burden of debt to help out with, but oh, my darling! If you'll just say that you think you might sometime in the future care for me I'll work like a fiend, and I'll get somewhere just as soon as I can where I can discharge all the responsibility and take care of you too. Do you think you could ever care?"

He held her off anxiously and searched her face in the semi-darkness, as the taxi whirled around the corner into Cromar Street.

"Oh," said Natalie softly, catching her breath, "I care *now*. I care with all my heart! It may sound dreadful, but I think I've cared ever since you were a boy in school and I used to love to listen to you reciting."

Then she hid her confusion against his coat, and they clung together.

It was only the taxi stopping in front of Natalie's home that brought them back to earth again.

Chris helped her out, and they made quite a promenade of the walk from the street to the porch, twelve feet by actual measurement.

"But I've got a family too, and responsibilities," said Natalie coming to her senses. "I couldn't—"

"Well, of course we couldn't now," said Chris slipping his arm about her and holding her close to his side. "But, with God's help we'll get where we can. I'll get where I can take care of my responsibilities and yours too, and then, you won't have to stay in a store and work any longer. A store—*our* store is all right of course," he added loyally—"but it isn't the place for the woman I love, you know, and I want you taken care of, my darling! And now, you ought to get right in and go to bed. I can feel you are trembling. Shall I go in and tell your mother what's happened?"

"No," said Natalie, "not to-night. It isn't necessary for her to know about that man—at all—maybe—. She doesn't go out much. She wouldn't be likely to hear it I hope. Because I'm afraid if she knew, she would be frightened every time I went to the store. And—about—*us,*—well, perhaps we'd better wait a little for that. She likes you a lot, but—it might seem sudden to her. We'll wait and talk it over a few days first, shall we?"

"I'd like that," said Chris. "It's like having our own secret a few minutes longer. But I mean everyone shall know it the first minute I'm in a position to take care of you. And I think we ought to tell your mother very soon."

Then suddenly he stooped and kissed her softly again.

"I'm only a poor girl you know," she reminded him. "I've been in another class from yours almost all my life."

"Thank God for that!" said Chris fervently, "if you hadn't been you might not have been willing to love me now. Oh, darling, I'm the happiest person alive I believe.

And to think God had this in store for me. Why, Natalie, I'm glad, glad of every hard thing that's happened to me when it brought me this beautiful love out of the darkness. Just think, if I'd gone back to college this last year I might never have known you at all, except as a quiet little girl in my high school class! And I was sore as could be that I had to give up my college. What's college beside a love like this?"

They might have talked all night if Janice hadn't come with brisk steps down the little narrow hall inside and flung the door wide open.

"What are you two doing out there in the cold?" she asked keenly. "Nice night for a tête à tête, isn't it, north-easter blowing forty knots an hour and you two aren't even aware of it. There'll be snow before morning, and Natalie took the old ratty fur off the neck of her coat this morning too. Come on in where it's warm. If you two want to talk secrets Mother and I will stay in the kitchen and you can have the front room."

Chris and Natalie looked up shamefacedly.

"Thank you, I'm just going," said Chris, "I have to get back to the store for a little while. I brought Natalie home. She was—a little tired—at least—she ought to be! She's—worked hard to-day."

"What was that car I heard stopping out here at the door a few minutes ago?" asked Janice sharply looking from one to the other of the two curiously.

"Oh, why, that was a taxi," explained Chris. "You see, I thought your sister was pretty tired, and there was a taxi—and so——" he finished lamely.

"Is my sister sick?" asked Janice lowering her voice so that it would not reach to the kitchen.

"Not in the least," said Natalie promptly and briskly. "It was just a notion. I'll tell you all about it, Jan, when we get up to bed. It was just—nothing."

"Is she sick?" asked Janice looking straight through Chris.

"No," said Chris smiling and facing her clear gaze. "Not a bit, only I think she's had a hard day and she ought to get to bed soon. That's honest, little sister, so run along and don't worry. I must go at once."

Janice grinned at him amicably.

"All right, big brother, I'll see that she gets to bed at once. Any tonic or anything needed?"

"No, just a glass of good milk and something hot to eat, and—I wouldn't worry Mother if I were you. She'll be all right." He smiled a wonderful radiance at Natalie, and Janice lost none of the radiance as she watched him.

"I still have my senses," said Janice caustically.

Chris took a reluctant leave, and Janice swung the door shut.

"He's getting very chummy! 'Little sister,' and 'Mother' indeed! Sounds almost like one of the family," and she grinned at Natalie. "Come on in, duck-of-a-sister, and eat supper. We thought you were never coming. There's only creamed codfish, but its delickety if I do say so, as-who-made-it, and there are plenty of fluffy boiled potatoes to eat with it, and cranberry sauce for dessert. Mother made that so you know it's all right. And Mother's interest money has come and it's five whole dollars more than it was last time, so there! Now, will you be good!"

Janice's manner was gaiety itself, but she gave her sister a keen glance, and decided that she must go early to bed.

Chris went back to the store so happy that he scarcely knew what he was about, and found himself quite a hero in the eyes of the whole police force, who hung around the store, kept him company, and talked the attempted burglary over so many times that it almost seemed like a great bank robbery by the time they had got done.

About half past eleven there came a wild ringing of the telephone. The manager had just got home and found the chief of police's message that something had happened at the store. He was wild with anxiety at once.

The chief happened still to be in the store, and lounged over to answer the call. The story had lost none of its spice in its many times telling, and Foster got a vivid description of the whole attempted robbery with full details, and plenty of credit for Natalie and Chris.

Then the manager wanted to speak to Chris, and was thankful almost to tears for what Chris had done. He said that he knew if anything had really been pulled off when he left the store in charge of someone else, that he would be blamed for it, and his managership probably taken from him, and it would mean losing all he had gained in five hard years of work in the store, from under-helper up. He declared he was coming right up even though it was late. He wanted to take Chris by the hand. He wanted to be on the spot and hear the whole account over again. No, he couldn't wait till morning, he was coming right away. Would Chris wait? It wouldn't take him long to get there in his car.

They had quite a session in the store at midnight. All the police force that could be spared for a few minutes from preventing other incidents that come under the law, were assembled. In fact they had spent most of the evening hovering about and trying to make a hero out of Chris. By the time the manager arrived Chris was getting almost bored with it.

"I didn't do anything much," he growled. "There wasn't anything else I could do, was there? It was just a matter of—" he was going to say "luck" but he hesitated and finished "It was just a little old miracle that I hit that gun, and that it didn't go off in Miss Halsey's face instead of on the floor. I was scared stiff as soon as I'd done it lest that was what had happened, and I could see the thing I ought to have done was send out a big alarm and scare the fellow away, only—well somehow I couldn't see having the bum get away, and try it on us again some time. He wasn't safe to have around, that guy."

So they praised him and slapped him on the back, and called him "Chris" adoringly and familiarly, and rallied around him till far after midnight.

He had telephoned early in the evening that he was detained at the store. But his mother had not been able to sleep till he came. She called to him softly as he came up the stairs:

"All right, Chris?"

"Sure, Mother!" he said pushing open her door and stepping in to put a kiss on her lips. Then he slipped out again with never a word about the excitement that had detained him.

When Chris finally got to his own room he was so excited it seemed to him he would never be able to sleep. He was so happy he did not know himself. After the months of sadness and doubt and darkness, the hard work and bitterness, here was so much joy handed out to him at once that he couldn't take it all in yet.

But above the kindly words of his manager, the praise of the whole police force, and the glow of pleasure in his heart that he had been able to save the store from loss, rang the sweetness of the thought that Natalie loved him, and the glad thanksgiving to God for letting him save her life.

"And she loves me! She loves me!" his heart sang as he prepared to turn in. "I know everybody would think I was a fool and all kinds of a cad to tell a girl I loved her when I haven't a cent to offer her, but please God I will have, and she understands. We'll just keep our own counsel and talk to God about it, and I'm sure the time won't be so far away when I can have the privilege of taking care of my dear girl."

Then for the first time in several years he knelt down and really prayed, thanking God for the way He had led him, and even for all the sorrow He had sent, which had brought such glory and joy into his life.

After that he lay down to his rest, but lay awake to think how sweet and shy Natalie had looked when she told him how she had cared for him even when he was a boy in High School. And he thrilled to the memory of the touch of her soft lips on his eyelids. Oh, Natalie was a wonderful girl! And she was going to be his some day! Life had suddenly taken on glory. Even hard work was glorious.

16

THE family read about it the next morning in the paper as they sat at breakfast, just after Chris had swallowed a bite or two and rushed away, and before Elise went off to school. Chris hadn't stopped to wait for the rest to come down. He said he had to be early at the store.

His fellow workmen met him with marked deference and respect, going out of their way to be nice to him. It made him feel like laughing. A hero he was, all for throwing a few green apples at a man's head instead of aiming a baseball at a mark. He laughed to himself as he went about his work of setting out the fresh vegetables that came in. What a little thing it took to make a hero after all, and why had he ever cared so much about it?

About ten o'clock the District Manager arrived and then it was all to do over again, the hero worship business. The District Manager had some stately words to say concerning the Company's indebtedness to him. It was quite public for there were even customers going around picking out heads of lettuce and oranges. They paused, all of them, and looked at Chris, and had to hear the story again from the quiet respectful salesmen who yearned to have been in Chris's boots last night. Albeit none of them had the reputation as a baseball pitcher that Chris had enjoyed in school, and each knew in his secret soul that he wouldn't have made half as good a showing as Chris had done in nabbing that bandit and saving the cashier's life.

Then the District Manager and the Manager called Chris and Natalie into the back room, and shut the door, and the District Manager told Natalie that the Company were greatly pleased with her service in saving the Company money and having presence of mind, and they were raising her salary and giving her a little platinum wrist watch with a suitable engraving to commemorate the event. He then turned to Chris and told him that the Company had been watching him with interest during his stay with them and had decided to give him a promotion with raise of salary in the near future, but that last night's good work had decided them to make the move at once. The Assistant Manager was moving to the coast, and the Company had decided to put Chris in his place. They wanted him to be in a position to learn as much as possible from Mr. Foster with a view to taking a managership himself some day. And of course there would be a substantial raise in his salary also.

Chris was overwhelmed. He tried to thank the Manager and the District Manager, and he broke down huskily. Then he and Natalie stood just like two children with their eyes full of gratitude. Chris's heart was swelling with pride.

That noon he took Natalie over to the tea room for lunch to celebrate. It was their first real chance to talk it all over alone, for last night they had been too engrossed with each other. But they could only sit and exclaim and beam at one another.

"You were *wonderful!*" said Natalie, her eyes filling

with tears in spite of her effort to keep them back. "You saved my life! He was going to shoot! I could see it in his eyes. He was furious!"

"Oh, my dear!" said Chris looking at her with something in his eyes that brought the color to her cheeks, "Oh, God was good! Oh, I'm glad, glad, now, that I didn't get to college, and that I was put just here to help save you. I suppose perhaps someone else would have saved you, if I hadn't been here, but I'm glad it was I instead of anyone else. And come to think of it, Natalie, if the bank hadn't closed, and Dad hadn't lost his money, I might never have known you."

They did not do much eating in that half hour of lunchtime, but they went back to their duties radiantly happy.

That night when Chris came in his family met him with open arms.

"So, son," said his father rising to meet him, "You've been making a hero of yourself. Got your picture in the paper and everybody calling up to tell me how fine you are."

"Picture in the paper!" said Chris disgusted, "How did they do that?"

"Oh, they raked up that old football snapshot, the one with your torn sweater on and mud on your face, the one the girls in school used to carry around in their school books," said his sister with dancing eyes. "Some brother I've got. Look! It's in the evening paper!"

"Good night!" said Chris modestly. "What a fuss about throwing a few apples!"

"Yes," said his father, "and that's not all. Mr. Mac-Laughlin called up this morning and offered to take you into the Title and Trust Company and train you into a banker. Title and Trust is a good old Company, solid as Gibraltar. How about it, Chris? Want to be a banker?"

But Chris shook his head.

"Nothing doing, Dad. They wouldn't have me when I needed it, and now I'm in line for managership of the chain store someday. I wouldn't give it up for any old job in a bank, not on a bet. I'd be years getting a pittance, and then some. Then there's another thing, a grocery is a good solid business. You can't have a run on a grocery. People have to eat. I'm sticking by the chain store. It's a great institution, and I'm throwing in my lot with them. Someday maybe I'll be the head of the whole company."

"But Chris, dear, a banker is always so much respected. Your father—"

"I know, Mother dear, it's a very respectable business, but so is the grocery business, and one banker is enough in the family at a time. Besides, Mother, I didn't notice that respect saved our home when we got in a tight place. Dad was one in a thousand of course, and everybody understood that and trusted him, but I didn't see that it got him by any better than if he'd been a grocer, and I'm putting my lot in with the chain store if you don't object."

"Of course not, son," said the father quickly, "Not if you've thought it over carefully and decided that way. I'm proud to have a son like you and the grocery business is good and honorable, and as much needed as a bank."

"Another thing, Mother," said Chris getting a little flustered, "I—we—I've about decided I want to get ready to do some real kind of Christian work in the world, and that takes money."

They were silent for very wonder, and Chris got red and embarrassed and looked down at his plate.

"You see we—that is I—I've come to see things in a different way lately. I used to think what you believed was mostly bunk. Yes, I did. Oh, I know I went to church and all that, but I thought it wasn't quite square when you and Dad believed so firmly in God for you to lose all you had. But now I see it differently, and I want to study the Bible and get ready to be of some use in the church and among people. I don't just know how to tell you," he floundered around searching for words, and was aware of his sister's bright eyes fixed upon him half mockingly.

"You see, we—that is, I—You see there's a girl, Mother, I'd like you to invite to dinner or something!" he blurted out.

"Chris!" said his mother instantly aghast, "Oh, Chris, you aren't trying to tell me that you want to get married. Not *yet?*"

Chris laughed excitedly.

"What do you think I am, Mother? Crazy? Of course not. But she's just a wonderful girl, and I want you to know her."

"And you haven't been getting engaged either?" she asked anxiously.

"Not exactly engaged, Mother, dearest, what have I got to get engaged on? I've got a family to look out for, and she has too. We've got to work hard, both of us for awhile yet—But we like each other a lot, Mother, and I want you to know her."

"Is she that girl whose life you saved, Chris?"

Chris looked her straight in the eye, his color rising a bit.

"Yes, Mother, if you call it that, though I'm not so sure she didn't save mine instead, calling up the police just in time."

She looked at him again a little uncertainly. Then a bright smile bloomed out.

"I'll go and see her to-morrow, Chris."

"Thanks, Mother, a lot. You'll like her I know."

"I'll try, anyway," said the mother bravely.

"You won't have to try, little Mother," sang Chris with a lilt in his voice and something gay and beautiful in his eyes, "She's wonderful! I know you'll like her, Mother. She's your kind!"

He stooped and kissed her tenderly.

"Well, I'm sure I hope for your sake that she is," she said with a quivery smile and a mother-sigh.

Chris went back to his chair again and tilted it back against the wall.

"There's another thing, folks," he said kicking the toes of his shoes gently together to hide his embarrassment. "You might as well hear the whole story at once."

They all looked up startled, but he did not give them time to worry.

"It's this. I've got to the place where I can say I'm glad, from my own standpoint, really glad all this trouble happened to us. I can see that going back to college and all that isn't always the best thing a fellow can have to begin his life with, and that whatever God hands out is always best. It's Natalie's doings. She's a wonderful Christian, folks, the kind of Christian you are, Mother; and she's made me see it too. She's had a lot of hard things in her life and she says she's glad for them; that they've helped her to know God better, and not be selfish and all that. And—well—she's got me thinking that too. And now I feel that I am really saved. I wasn't before, but now I am, and I want God to have His way in my life. And—we—we're going to study the Bible, evenings, at a class that's been started down at the Water Street Mission. I just thought I'd like to have you know the whole thing."

But his father was on his feet now, standing beside him looking down with shining eyes, and his mother came over and laid her lips tenderly on his hair where it fell away from his forehead.

Then his father spoke:

"Chris, dear son, that's the best thing you ever told me. That's better than health or wealth or anything else in life. To know that you belong to Christ and are learning to be led by His will. I have known all along that God was handing us His best when He sent sorrow and humiliation and scorn and poverty for me and mine, but I didn't see why He did it and I didn't expect to see why till I got over in the Home Eternal. But He has made me see, now, bless His Holy name! I'm glad He gave us trouble when it was to lead to such a great joy as this. And we'll love the little girl too, for having helped."

"Yes, dear!" said the mother, making it like a promise.

"Well, then, that's all right!" sighed Chris with joy in his face, getting up and walking gaily around the room. "I ought to have known you'd take it like this, but I hated like the dickens to tell you. I wasn't sure I could make you understand."

"You can always make us understand, son, when you use the language of heaven," said his father with a wonderful smile. "I'd rather have you tell me what you just did than anything else in the world. I'd rather have you know the Lord than be the richest banker that ever lived."

So presently, Chris kissed them all around, pinched his sister's cheek to make her look less solemn, and hurried away to the next street to call on Natalie.

But it was really Natalie's mother that he called on first. He found her sitting in the front room finishing a bit of sewing while the girls washed the supper dishes. He went over and took her work gently out of her hands and laid it carefully on the table as she looked up wonderingly at him with a half premonition in her eyes.

"Now, Mother Halsey," he said as tenderly as he would have spoken to his own mother, "I've come to confess to you. I don't know what you will say to me, and I'm sorry if you don't like it, but it's done and you ought to know about it. You see last night I told Natalie that I loved her. I didn't mean to do it so soon, not till I had an assured position in life and plenty of money to take care of her the way she ought to be taken care of. But—well—I—we— Well, I *told* her, and I found out she cares too, and I thought you ought to know it. I don't want to do anything underhanded. Do you mind, very much, Mother Halsey?"

Natalie's mother looked at the earnest young man who was waiting so eagerly for her answer, her lip trembled, and tears welled into her eyes, but she said with a real smile and a bit of a quiver in her voice:

"You dear boy!" and then she put up her two hands and softly laid them one on each of his cheeks and drew him toward her and kissed him gently.

Then she whisked out her handkerchief, brushed away the tears, and smiled again.

"I ought to be very glad and proud," she said, "I *am*. Of course it is a little bit sudden, and you are both young, and I was afraid of a rich young man at first. I didn't know how dear you were—"

Her lip quivered again.

"But I'm not rich, Mother Halsey," Chris laughed joyously, "I'm poor as a church mouse. That's what makes it so bad for me to have told Natalie how I feel when I can't do a thing about it yet, but if you'll trust me I'll work hard, and try to get to a place where I can give her the kind of home she ought to have."

"Oh I meant you were accustomed to riches. I was afraid you would be spoiled,—you may as well know the truth! But you're not! You're all and more than I could possibly desire in a man for my dear girl. And I'm proud of you besides. Oh, I've read the papers. You and Natalie thought you had kept last night's happenings from me, and Janice helped too, but the boy that came to fix the gas stove told me, and showed me a paper. He knew who Natalie was, and who you were, and I know all about it, and I'm proud of you both. Of course I didn't expect this—that is not so soon anyway—but I guess you had a right—and I can understand."

"You're a peach, little new mother," said Chris, "and I hope I shan't disappoint you. The only thing is I wish I could get Natalie out of that store right away, though of course I'd miss the sight of her greatly. But I'd like to relieve her and all of you at once of all care and work."

"Well, that's dear of you. But of course Natalie must go on working, and you mustn't expect to have all you want right away. It won't hurt either of you to work and win your way ahead, and I'm glad that Natalie has a real joy in her life. She's never had much chance to have a good time—"

"Now, Mother!" protested Natalie, from the kitchen doorway, "I've always had a happy life."

"Yes, you've been a good girl and said so," smiled the mother half ruefully.

"No, but Mother, I have!" insisted Natalie, "I've been happy in my home and family. I've had you and Father and my wonderful sister."

"Yes, she would add that," said Janice joining them as she wafted a dish towel over the dinner plates. "She's some sister, I tell you, big brother!"

"You've said it!" added Chris earnestly. "Say, I'm so happy I could swing my hat in the air and shout!"

"But," warned the mother, "you may have a long road ahead full of disappointment and waiting, you know."

"We know," said Natalie smiling, "and we don't care. We have each other now, and those other things won't matter so much."

"And it's not going to be so frightfully long either, Mother Halsey, if I can make it short by hard work, see? And I guess it makes some difference, too, that we both belong to God, now, doesn't it?" he added shyly.

"It certainly does," said the mother with shining eyes. "It makes all the difference in the world to me. I couldn't have given my child to a man that didn't know the Lord you know, rich or poor. Natalie told me about that last night, and I certainly was glad, for of course I couldn't help seeing how things might be going, and should have been terribly troubled to have my girl going around with you much longer if you didn't belong to the Royal Family."

He flashed her a bright smile as she slipped out of the room and left him with Natalie.

"Oh, I'm glad I belong!" he said as Natalie came over to sit down beside him on the little old couch, and he took her hand, reverently, and bent over to lay his lips upon it.

But out in the kitchen Janice was complaining.

"I don't see, Mother, why they need to have the door shut. We are entirely in sympathy with them. Aren't they going to be chummy any more? If I were you I wouldn't begin that way."

"Well, Janice," smiled the mother, "suppose you let them have a little chance to talk things over first. We'll make a bit of fudge and the smell of it'll call them out by and by. There's fresh chocolate that Natalie brought home to-night. Suppose you start it while I finish this seam, and then I'll help stir it."

And so presently the enticing smell of cooking chocolate stole silently under the crack of the front room door, and brought the two back to earth again from the little earthly heaven they had been planning sometime in the future, and they came out with shining eyes and helped beat the fudge, turn by turn, till Chris claimed the right to finish it all himself.

After Chris was gone home that night Janice turned back with a satisfied sigh:

"Well, I guess it's going to be nice after all, having a brother-in-law. He seems to be able to tune in pretty well anywhere, and anyway my arm always does ache stirring fudge!"

IT was a bright day in the following spring that Chris brought his father down to the bank in an old second hand Ford he had bought for a song; for the Fidelity Bank and Trust Company had opened its doors again to the public, and was rewarded by a long line of depositors waiting to put back into the bank the money they had recently received from it.

The bank had been able to pay back every cent of its indebtedness and to get on its feet again for business with a clean record.

It had been nothing short of a miracle that had made this all possible, and the one who had been used to work this miracle was Christopher Walton, senior, the honored president. For he had been unanimously elected president again, even against his own protest. The bank felt that it could not do without his influence and good judgment. They recognized that it had been largely through his wisdom and efforts that the marvelous reconstruction of the bank's affairs had been brought about.

Two things had conspired to make possible this

miracle of the business world. Three men, warm friends of Mr. Walton's who had been in Europe at the time of the closing of the bank's doors, had returned, and come to the aid of the bank with a large sum of money; this, added to the fact that Mr. Walton had been able to turn over at a good figure, a huge block of real estate in which much of the bank's assets had been tied up, had restored the people's confidence, and the bank was in a fair way to be stronger than ever.

Mr. Walton's personal fortune was of course gone, but he had his friends and his business, and the confidence of his neighbors once more.

"And some day," said Chris Junior, as they talked it over one night, "you might even be able to buy back our home, that is when I get to be owner of the chain stores of course," and he grinned. "I love that place and so does Natalie, and I'd like to have it back and see you and Mother in it again. I heard the other day that the chump that bought it is getting restive again and seeking fairer pastures. He says the people in this town are all a set of highhats and he thinks he'll go to Europe and buy an old palace somewhere in Italy. When he does I mean to see what can be done toward buying it back. That is, of course, if God is willing," he added softly half under his breath. "What He wants goes with me from now on."

Mr. Foster had been transferred to the managership of the district and Chris was now manager of the store. He was as pleased as if he had been made president of the United States, perhaps even more pleased, for he had developed a genuine love for his store and the goods he handled. His efficiency had been noticed and commended more than once from headquarters.

"Meantime, Dad," went on Chris after a minute, "I've been thinking. I find this house next to us here is on the market at a ridiculously low price and I'm talking with the agent about financing it. He thinks it can be done at a price that I could carry perhaps. What would you think about it? It's a double house you know, and it has possibilities. We could do a lot of little things ourselves to it, and I just thought, if Natalie and I found it possible pretty soon to get married, we could take this side and let Natalie's mother and Jan have the other side, and then we families would all be together. At least that would do for the present till we could manage to get back the old home."

"I think it would be lovely!" said Mrs. Walton quickly, her eyes sparkling. "That won't be like losing you. Oh, Chris, you're a darling boy!"

"Well, Mother dear, that was Natalie's suggestion. She loves you, she really does, and her mother does too."

"And I love them both, and Janice too," the mother added, "and so does your father and Elise. I think we are going to be very happy, whether we get the old house back or not. I'm not sure but I'd be just as well satisfied to stay right here. It's cozy, and we're all happy together."

That was the beginning of the talk, but things moved rapidly on, and it wasn't long before the house next door was getting a new coat of paint and paper outside and in. Natalie was shopping for some very cheap pretty bargain curtains, and evenings were exciting times when everybody had to come over to the new house and see the latest thing that had been done to it.

It was Betty Zane's young sister that asked Elise one day:

"Say, Elise, is it true that your brother is going to marry that Halsey girl?"

"Yes," said Elise coldly, "it is." Her tone did not invite

further comment, but her smile showed that she was entirely satisfied with his choice.

"Mercy," said the other girl disagreeably, "did she work in a store? I should think you'd feel terribly about it."

"Yes, she worked in a store," said Elise proudly, "and so does my brother, but we are just delighted about it. We love her very dearly and are very glad that he is going to marry her. She's choice. Good-by, I'm going down this way to-day," and Elise swept around the corner a trifle haughtily.

But it was some weeks later that Betty Zane and Anna Peters were walking down the street together.

"Did you know," began Betty, "that Chris Walton and that quiet little mouse of a Natalie Halsey are being married this evening? The wedding is in the church, and only a few intimate friends are invited. But they say the owner of the chain stores is coming, and that he gave Natalie a whole silver service. Aren't things queer? Chris Walton working in a grocery store and then getting to be manager. But I can't understand his marrying that poor little Halsey girl."

"I heard she came of a fine old family," said Anna.

"Well, what's that when you haven't a rag to wear on your back? I wonder what on earth she'll wear to be married in? Something old or made over I'll bet."

"Well yes, it's old, and it'll be made over a little perhaps," laughed Anna disagreeably. "Our dressmaker is doing it. But she says it's gorgeous. It's her mother's wedding dress, ivory satin, and a thread lace veil that must have cost a fabulous price. Natalie's almost her mother's size. The dress hardly has to be changed at all, just taken in a little on the shoulders. I think she might have invited us, don't you? Her old school mates! They say she has some gorgeous presents from the people in the stores. I'd like to see them. I think it was real mean of her not to ask us."

"Well," soliloquized Betty, "I don't quite see why she should. We never acted as if we knew she existed when she was in school. But I suppose now that Mr. Walton is back in the bank and everything going prosperously we'll have to take her up."

"I don't see why," said Anna. "They're going to live down on that little old Sullivan Street. Isn't it queer, when they don't have to any more? I don't see why they should expect us to call on them."

"Well, if you ask me," said Betty's younger sister, "I don't believe they know or care what you do. They live in a world of their own and they like it. I've been talking with Janice Halsey a lot lately and she says they all go down to that Water Street mission and study the Bible. I think they're all *queer*."

"Yes," said Anna sighing half wistfully, "I guess that's it. They're just peculiar people. They don't seem to mind in the least that they lost all their money and had to go and live down there in that unfashionable district. Fancy staying there when they don't have to! And I guess they are happy, for I met Chris the other day and he was whistling away, and he smiled at me like a beam of sunshine, though I know he can't bear me. I just can't understand it. They are happier than they were when they were rich. And those Halseys seem happy too."

"I know," said Betty. "I don't understand it. They're happy without things, and I've got a lot and sometimes I'm awfully bored with life. Wouldn't you think they'd just be desperate to think they had all that money and that lovely home and had to give it up? And yet they go around looking as if they'd just inherited a fortune and belonged to a royal family."

Five blocks away from where those girls were walking Chris was fingering a delicate wedding ring on Natalie's finger and saying:

"Natalie, I've been thinking how wonderful God has been to us, to just take me out of the life I was living that I thought was so wonderful and put me where I might know you. Oh, you darling!"

## About the Author

Grace Livingston Hill is well known as one of the most prolific writers of romantic fiction. Her personal life was fraught with joys and sorrows not unlike those experienced by many of her fictional heroines.

Born in Wellsville, New York, Grace nearly died during the first hours of life. But her loving parents and friends turned to God in prayer. She survived miraculously, thus her thankful father named her Grace.

Grace was always close to her father, a Presbyterian minister, and her mother, a published writer. It was from them that she learned the art of storytelling. When Grace was twelve, a close aunt surprised her with a hardbound, illustrated copy of one of Grace's stories. This was the beginning of Grace's journey into being a published author.

In 1892 Grace married Fred Hill, a young minister, and they soon had two lovely young daughters. Then came 1901, a difficult year for Grace—the year when, within months of each other, both her father and husband died. Suddenly Grace had to find a new place to live (her home was owned by the church where her husband had been pastor). It was a struggle for Grace to raise her young daughters alone, but through everything she kept writing. In 1902 she produced *The Angel of His Presence, The Story of a Whim,* and *An Unwilling Guest.* In 1903 her two books *According to the Pattern* and *Because of Stephen* were published.

It wasn't long before Grace was a well-known author, but she wanted to go beyond just entertaining her readers. She soon included the message of God's salvation through Jesus Christ in each of her books. For Grace, the most important thing she did was not write books but share the message of salvation, a message she felt God wanted her to share through the abilities he had given her.

In all, Grace Livingston Hill wrote more than one hundred books, all of which have sold thousands of copies and have touched the lives of readers around the world with their message of "enduring love" and the true way to lasting happiness: a relationship with God through his Son, Jesus Christ.

In an interview shortly before her death, Grace's devotion to her Lord still shone clear. She commented that whatever she had accomplished had been God's doing. She was only his servant, one who had tried to follow his teaching in all her thoughts and writing.

If you are unable to find any of these titles at your local bookstore, you may call Tyndale's toll-free number **1-800-323-9400, X-214** for ordering information. Or you may write for pricing to **Tyndale Family Products, P.O. Box 448, Wheaton, IL 60189-0448.**